A Heart Reclaimed

by Elizabeth Maddrey

www.ElizabethMaddrey.com

Cover design by Elizabeth Maddrey.
Cover art photos ©iStockphoto.com/photosbyandy, ©shutterstock.com/antonioguillem, ©shutterstock.com/sofiaworld used by permission.

Published in the United States of America by Elizabeth Maddrey
www.ElizabethMaddrey.com

Other Books by Elizabeth Maddrey

The 'Peacock Hill Romance' Series
A Heart Restored
A Heart Reclaimed

Arcadia Valley Romance – Baxter Family Bakery
Series
Loaves & Wishes (in *Romance Grows in Arcadia
Valley*)
Muffins & Moonbeams
Cookies & Candlelight (September 2017)
Donuts & Daydreams (March 2018)

The 'Operation Romance' Series
Operation Mistletoe
Operation Valentine
Operation Fireworks
Operation Back-to-School

The 'Taste of Romance' Series
A Splash of Substance
A Pinch of Promise
A Dash of Daring
A Handful of Hope
A Tidbit of Trust

The 'Grant Us Grace' Series
Joint Venture
Wisdom to Know
Courage to Change
Serenity to Accept

The 'Remnants' Series:
Faith Departed
Hope Deferred
Love Defined

Stand alone novellas
Kinsale Kisses: An Irish Romance

Non-Fiction
A Walk in the Valley: Christian encouragement
for your journey through infertility

For the most recent listing of all my books, please
visit my website.

For anyone who's ever needed a second chance at love.

1

Anna Hamilton parked her car under one of the shaggy cedars near the front of Peacock Hill and rubbed her hands together. Finally, a chance to be part of a project that mattered. Not that the historical landscape archives weren't important, but who wanted to be stuck behind a desk helping researchers when she could get her hands in the dirt? She couldn't really pinpoint how she'd ended up at the library, either. Which just made it worse. But now...maybe her life was back on track.

Gathering her laptop bag and her duffel, she stepped out of the car and breathed in the unpolluted air. It was lovely. Very little humidity and still cooler than Richmond, which was beginning to feel the first tendrils of Virginia summer weather. Even if it was barely May. She closed the car door and crossed the gravel drive, climbing the steps to the front of the house two at a time while she admired the columns and general grandeur of the place.

Anna knocked on the door. Would anyone hear if they weren't close by? The house—there had to be a better word. Mansion? Estate?—was massive.

"Coming." Footsteps clomped closer before the door swung open. The tiny blonde grinned and extended her hand. "Anna, right? I'm Deidre."

"That's me. Nice to meet you." Anna took her hand and peered inside. Rich wood—on the floor and the walls—met her gaze. "Gosh, it's even prettier in real life."

"Come on in. Is that all you brought?"

"I have more out in the car—you said to be prepared to rough it, so there's an air mattress and that kind of thing, too. I just wasn't sure..."

Deidre grinned. "I've got an actual mattress for you. It's on the floor, but it's better than a blow up. We're roughing it, but not quite at the camping level. You and I are on the second floor. I stuck my brother on the third."

"Sounds good."

Deidre paused and angled her head to the side.

Anna raised her brows. "What?"

"It's just...I want to make sure you didn't think you were in charge of the project?"

Anna worked to control the expression on her face. She *had* actually, but diplomacy was always a good idea. "Well, you have final say, of course."

Deidre shook her head. "I was afraid of that. I'm so sorry. See, my brother's a landscape architect and I asked him—practically as soon as I bought the place—to help out. I wasn't sure he'd be able to get down here this spring though, which is why I started looking around for photos and such—to see if I could do a little cleanup while I waited for him to have time. But his work schedule cleared up and he got here yesterday."

"I see." Although she didn't. Anna gripped the handle of her duffel. Three months of email and phone calls with Deidre had made her seem like a friend, of sort. Why had the woman never mentioned a brother? A landscaping brother at that. "So...you don't actually need me?"

"I didn't say that. I...it's just..." Deidre broke off and turned at the noise on the staircase.

"Hey, Dee, I was thinking...oh." A tall, sandy-haired man stopped on the steps, his features sliding into a blank mask. "Hello, Anna."

"McIntyre. Of course." Anna's stomach twisted into an entire batch of pretzels as she realized just who Deidre's brother was. She swallowed, willing some moisture into the desert of her mouth. "I should be going. Your project is in good hands."

Deidre shot Duncan a meaningful look.

Anna turned and reached for the door.

"I never figured you for one who'd walk away from a challenge."

Anna spun, scowling, as Duncan crossed the foyer. "You'd dare?"

"I'll just leave the two of you to work this out." Deidre patted Duncan's arm and beat a hasty retreat up the stairs.

"It's good to see you." He tucked his hands into his pockets with a cocky smile. "What's it been, ten years?"

Anna sucked a breath through her teeth. Up close it was clear none of her prayers had been answered since

Duncan wasn't balding, pockmarked, or obese. Preferably all three. He was even better looking than he'd been in college, if that was possible. The lanky young man had filled out—in all the right places—and what had been an attractive package was now deadly. "Something like that, yes. Look. I didn't realize she was your sister or I never would've come. Obviously you're more than capable of handling the gardens here after working at Marshall Brothers. I'm surprised they'd let you take the spring off."

He shrugged. "It's more of a leave of absence, to be honest."

"What? You have too many awards to fit in your office, so they sent you away while they built you a new one?" Not that she'd been following his career. Much. He just happened to get written up in all the magazines she enjoyed reading. Needed to read for professional development.

"Not quite." He sighed. "There's been some turnover at the top and I'm not sure I like the new direction they're heading. So, I took some time. Besides, this place? Who wouldn't want to work on it?"

Anna grinned before she could stop it. That was her thought, exactly. "Yes, well. You won this one, too. I'll let you get to it."

"Anna." His voice was quiet. Almost tender. A lot like it had been the last time she'd told him goodbye.

She blinked back the tears that filled her eyes. "What?"

"You're welcome to stay. I could use the help."

Her heart lifted, but she fought it. Trusting Duncan was as risky as planting in mid-January. "What's the catch?"

"Nothing, really. Except that I'm in charge."

He was in charge. Of *course* he was in charge. Duncan McIntyre was always in charge—even when he wasn't supposed to be. How many projects had they been on together, and the team had all looked to him, even when her ideas were better? Or at least as good. She sighed and kicked the corner of the mattress in the room Deidre had shown her to once she and Duncan had come to an understanding of sorts. It was clean and private. That was about all it had going. The bathroom was down the hall, shared with Deidre...and she shouldn't be complaining. She hadn't been summarily dismissed, and that was enough. Or it had the potential to be enough. A project like this was a huge opportunity to get her portfolio going. And she *had* to do something to get away from the archives. Her soul died a little every day she went in to work.

Duncan McIntyre.

Anna sank to the mattress and buried her head in her hands. Could she do this? She had the skills—and the knowledge of what used to be here. The question was, did

Deidre want a recreation of what had been or something new?

A tap at the door brought her to her feet. "Come in."

Deidre poked her head in. "Hey. You okay?"

"Yeah. Settling in, I guess." Anna glanced around the sparse room again, noting the presence of a desk and dresser for the first time. How had she missed those? Too absorbed with Duncan. And that needed to stop. "Did you need me?"

"I thought maybe you'd like to take a tour of the gardens? Talk about what I'm hoping for?"

"Of course." Anna dug through her bag for a notepad and pen. After a moment's hesitation, she grabbed the folder that had her collected research on Peacock Hill. "Lead on."

Deidre cleared her throat. "Actually...Duncan's waiting for you in the sunken garden at the right side of the house. Um, right as you exit the front door."

"Got it. Duncan." Her fingers curled around the pen. "I guess I shouldn't keep him waiting."

Deidre stepped aside as Anna strode into the hallway. "Wait."

Anna turned, her eyebrow raised.

"I don't know the history between you and my brother—it's clear there is some—but, he's really not a bad guy."

Anna nodded. That much was true. He'd been a good guy in college, too. It wasn't his fault she'd been half in love with him since the first day they met. Maybe it was his fault that he'd never noticed her, unless it was to steamroll over her ideas, but then again, she hadn't been what one would call assertive in college. At least that was something that time had changed. "I should go."

She hurried down the stairs, forcing herself not to gawk at the amazing stained glass window at the landing. There'd be time for that later. When Duncan wasn't waiting on her. Stepping out the front doors, she paused, just for a second, to gaze at the view of the Blue Ridge Mountains that rose in the distance. Technically, Peacock Hill was in the foothills, but seeing the mountains on the horizon still left her with a need to stop and soak them in. God had sure known what He was doing when He made this part of Virginia.

After giving herself a firm mental shake, she hurried down the steps and around the side of the house.

Duncan knelt at the base of a statue in the center of the sunken garden. He had something in his hand—a tool of some sort—and was using it to poke at the sculpture. The fountain was shaped like a fish standing on its tail. Presumably water was supposed to spout from its mouth into the pool at the bottom. Detail was lost under moss and grime, but Anna had a photo of it in her files that helped her see what could be again. She cleared her throat.

Duncan sat back on his heels. "Hey. I think I can probably get this working again. That's nice to know. You settled in?"

"I guess. Your sister said you wanted to see me?"

His eyebrows shot up. "I didn't mean it quite like that. I just asked if she'd let you know I was out here when you were settled. I thought we could take a tour and I'd run through what I had in mind and you can let me know where that's different from what was originally here."

"Because?"

"What do you mean?"

Anna sighed and hugged her folder and notebook to her chest. "Do you want to know because you want to restore it, or just so you can say 'How nice' and then do something else entirely?"

"Is this about our senior project?"

"Of course not." Was it? That would be...stupid. "Maybe."

His grin flashed. "Would it help if I apologized again? I wasn't trying to overrule you constantly. Your ideas were good. I simply happened to have a little inside info on the client and knew what she wanted."

And he'd been right, too. Another team had proposed something similar to the suggestions she'd made and been torn apart. The client had gone on to hire Duncan's team to make the proposal a reality. It had been a feather in all three of their caps. Even if it had hurt to know her ideas weren't worthy. "And now? It's the same, isn't it? If anyone was going to know what your sister wants, it'd be you."

"True. But as it happens, she wants a restoration as close as possible to the original. So I'd been planning to hit up the archives and see if there were photos or articles. Then Deidre told me she'd already been in touch and that someone was coming out." He stood and tucked his hands in his pockets. "Like I said earlier, I could use your help."

"Okay. Sorry." She came down the three steps into the sunken garden and looked around. The planting beds around the perimeter were overgrown and tangled with weeds and vines. Moss covered all the marble tiles that made up the patio floor. But the balustrade around the top of the wall was in good shape. If Duncan could get the fountain working again and they could dig up some wrought iron benches and paint them white, this part of the restoration would mostly require a lot of elbow grease. "You really think you can get the fish working?"

He nodded. "Yeah. I found the access panel in the column. The plumbing all looks good—at least what I can see—so either there's a leak, or, maybe it has a different shutoff that needs to be turned on."

"Or both."

"Sure. That's possible. You have any pictures of this area? I imagine it's fairly simple. Just the planted beds—maybe an urn or two up by the house since there's no planting area there?"

Anna pulled her gaze away from Duncan's. It was entirely too easy to get lost in those deep blue eyes. She swallowed. Not going down that path again. She was over him. She flipped open the folder and sifted through the papers. "Um. Pretty sure...yeah, here."

Duncan took the page she offered and held it out in front of him. "Any idea what these are? They could be azaleas. Hard to tell in this picture."

"I think they are, actually. Here." Anna handed him another photo. This one was a closer shot of a woman sitting in front of one of the bushes. The tell-tale azalea flower was much easier to spot. "If you didn't want to stick completely true to a restoration, planting a stand of bamboo, properly contained in a bucket so it doesn't take over, in each corner might add an interesting feel. Or some pampas grass."

"That would be nice. Break up the height some." He pulled his phone out of his pocket and tapped before turning to look at the side of the house. Was he taking notes? "What about urns? I think we need something there to break up the massive wall of stone."

"No photos from that angle." Anna closed her folder and considered the space. "What about a raised, rectangular planter in the middle instead? Or...well, if your sister would go for it, maybe a hanging planter attached to the wall with something viney and flowery dripping from it?"

"You always had a good eye. I'll ask—but I can't imagine why she'd mind." Duncan tapped on his phone again then slid it back into his pocket. "Ready to move on?"

"Sure. Lead the way." Anna took a deep breath and willed her fluttering stomach to settle. It couldn't—wouldn't—matter that Duncan was still the only man who made her pulse race. This was business.

2

Duncan took the steps out of the sunken garden two at a time. Anna Hamilton. How had he not figured out that's who Deidre meant when she said she'd found someone who'd done her thesis on Gilded Age gardens, including Peacock Hill, and had photos? But they'd been out of school for ten years—surely there were other, more recent students who'd done the same? The gardens of that period were worth studying. Had he even known that was Anna's topic? By the time they'd gotten around to choosing a thesis topic, he'd been convinced she hated him. And since all he'd wanted to do was ask her on a date, knowing there was no possible chance she'd agree had made him avoid her whenever possible.

Footsteps crunched on the gravel driveway behind him. He stopped and waited as Anna caught up.

"Wow."

Duncan nodded. "That was my first response, too. Have you ever seen a fountain like this?"

"No. It's like something from Rome. There weren't any pictures of this. Why weren't there photos? It's incredible."

He smiled. It was. Across the driveway, centered with the porte coché, the fountain must have been impressive to visitors as they arrived. The marble slabs stood eight feet tall, and the water feature itself was nearly as long as the house. There was a lion's head carved in the center panel from which water was, most likely, supposed to flow. Each of the side panels held bas relief flower arrangements. The pool at the bottom was only six inches deep, but the blue glazed tile would make the water look deeper.

"Can you fix it, too?"

"I haven't looked yet. I hope so. Something like this needs to be preserved. If I can't, I'll have to call around and see if I can find someone who can. Unless you know of someone who'd come out this way?"

"I...might? I'd have to think."

"I'll give it a look first. No plantings here, obviously. But the formal garden is up the steps on either side." Duncan pointed to the stairs and gestured for her to go ahead. That way he wouldn't walk too fast for her. Plus, it wasn't a hardship to follow behind her. Not that she seemed any more likely to accept a date with him now than she had been in college.

He climbed the stairs and nearly ran into her at the top.

"This is sad." Anna took a step into the overgrown space and turned. "How long was it neglected?"

"Deidre isn't sure. The owner was getting old. Hadn't lived here for several years, though supposedly the kids were taking care of things. Maybe that just meant they were checking it hadn't burned down. Either way, it worked out well for my sister to be able to invest the money she got from settling a contract dispute." Duncan put his hands on his hips and looked out over the tangle of weeds in front of him. "I'll admit, I'm not exactly sure what this area is supposed to be."

Anna's face lit and she reached into her folder again. "Look."

The photo was black and white, but it still clearly showed the formal garden as it had once been. Paths defined geometric shapes among planting beds filled with blooms. Hedges lined the perimeter, creating two separate, almost cozy spaces. In the center of each was a fountain. Duncan frowned. "I don't think the water features are still there."

"Let's walk through and see." Anna took the photo back and put it in her folder.

Duncan pushed through the overgrowth. There was a lot of work to be done here to clear the pathways. Several would need regrading. All would need fresh gravel. And that was before the planting beds. Those...would need to simply be torn out and replanted from scratch. Should he move down here permanently? Deidre frequently begged him to do so. He hadn't told anyone—including his employer—but the decision was a definite possibility.

"No fountain." Anna kicked at a slightly raised hump of earth. "This has to be where it goes. But...it's been gone for a while."

"We can ask Deidre if she wants us to put some kind of water feature back. Looking at this, we're going to be tearing up everything and starting fresh."

Anna propped her hands on her hips. "I guess. That's certainly going to be the easiest choice."

"What would you do?"

She shrugged. "Some of those plants might be close to a hundred years old. I think they deserve to have a shot."

Duncan shook his head. There was no way the plants in these overgrown nightmares was what a gardener put there originally. "Doubtful. They're weeds."

"I just think it's worth having a look first, before you bring in a backhoe and dig everything up."

"Fine. Tell you what, why don't you go ahead and poke through the mess up here? I'll get you some markers to tie around any of the plants you think are worth saving." Two ought to be about twice as many as she'd need.

"Perfect." Anna crossed her arms. "Was there more to this tour or are we done?"

"I think that's enough for today." Shaking his head, Duncan turned and stalked through the dead garden and down the steps. He paused at the side of the wall fountain and frowned. What was with her, anyway?

"Hey. Done with the tour already?" Deidre set down her sanding block and pulled the dust mask off, leaving it to dangle around her neck.

"Apparently." Duncan stuck his hands in the pockets of his jeans and looked around the dining room. "It's looking nice in here."

"Thanks." She grinned. "The adhesive product for plaster repair is a lot easier than the old way with screws. And, theoretically, it should hold longer. But sanding is still for the birds."

"You'd have to sand either way though, right?"

"Yeah, yeah." Deidre stuck out her tongue. "Are you going to be able to work with Anna? I didn't realize you two had a history."

From the light in her eyes and the angle of her head, she was fishing. It was the same look she'd used to ferret out who he wanted to ask to the prom when he was in high school. "There's no history. We went to school together."

"At Tech? Cool."

He shrugged. "She doesn't seem much different. Still opinionated and determined she's right about everything. Which means I'm heading into town to see if that little hardware store has something that'll work as a marker in case she finds a hundred-year-old treasure when she's sorting through the planting beds of the formal garden."

"I thought you were just going to scrape it all off and go from there?"

"Yeah? So did I." Duncan turned and started toward the doorway.

"Hey."

He stopped and looked back.

"You're in charge, remember. Just tell her no."

He shook his head. "Might as well let her have her way on this one. Maybe she'll let me handle the pond behind the arbor."

Deidre wrinkled her nose. "That's no pond. It's just a low spot where water collects into a stagnant mess."

"By the time I'm done with it, it'll be a pond."

"I was hoping we could put in a swimming pool in for the guests."

Duncan pursed his lips. A pool. It was a good idea. But it needed to go somewhere that made sense. "I'll find you a spot. Write down what you're thinking, size-wise. Oh—there might have been fountains at the center of each side of the formal gardens, too. Do you want those put back?"

"Is there anything left?"

"Just a little hill. They've been gone a while."

Deidre shook her head. "Then no. There are enough things spewing water around here."

Duncan grinned. "You talk like you have no romance in you, but I've seen you with Jeremiah."

Pink stole across her cheeks. "Go away. I need to sand this plaster if I'm going to stay on schedule."

Laughing, his heart lighter, Duncan strode through the foyer and out the front door to his car. Maybe the hardware store would have what he needed to repair the fountains in the sunken gardens, too. Never hurt to look.

3

Anna sat back on her heels and rolled her head on her shoulders. She glanced back over the progress she'd made since she started Tuesday afternoon and sighed. There hadn't been one salvageable plant yet. Which probably had Duncan chortling to himself every night. At least he hadn't said anything the few times they'd bumped into each other. Should she just give up and concede defeat?

"Hey." Deidre jogged over to Anna and held out a water bottle before she sat on the overgrown grass and unscrewed the lid on her own. "How's it going?"

Anna shrugged. "Nothing yet. I was just wondering if maybe I should give it up."

"How much is left?"

"I'm nearly done with this side—maybe another two hours should see me through. But I haven't even started on the other one." Anna twisted the lid off the bottle and took a long drink. Her own water had grown warm as she worked and, while she forced herself to keep drinking, this water was icy and refreshing as it slid down her throat.

"Got plans for the weekend?"

Anna pointed to the overgrown area of the garden. "Did you miss where I said I hadn't started over there yet?"

"Okay, sure. You can put in a few hours tomorrow. I'll probably try and get the first coat of primer up in the breakfast room. But what about tonight? Or tomorrow night? Sunday?"

Anna put the lid back on and rolled the bottle between her palms. "I'll find a church on Sunday morning. And maybe go for a hike in the afternoon. I've always loved the hikes off Skyline Drive, and since it's close...but otherwise I'm here to work. I don't see the point in doing anything else."

"Okay. Well, if you change your mind, you're welcome to join us for dinner tonight. Jeremiah's bringing pizza after he finishes up in Waynesboro, and some of his friends will probably join us. Same for tomorrow night, although it's not likely to be pizza. Maybe we can talk Jeremiah into making nachos. His are killer."

Anna's stomach quivered. What was the right answer? From the few interactions she'd had with Deidre, Anna had decided they could be friends under the right circumstances. But those didn't include having her brother be Duncan. Which wasn't likely to change. So the friend thing was purely hypothetical. But a long evening in her room watching TV on her tablet while laughter floated up the stairs from people having fun on the main floor didn't appeal either. She took another long drink of water, emptying the bottle. "I'll see how I feel. Okay?"

Deidre gave her a long look before nodding. "Sure. I hope you join us. Want me to take that bottle back in and recycle it?"

"Yeah. Thanks."

Deidre stood and dusted off the back of her jeans. "Seriously, there's going to be plenty of food. So don't try to use that as an excuse not to come."

Anna smiled and turned back to the weeds. Plenty of food and Duncan. Would he be the charming, easy-to-get-along-with man she'd glimpsed during their tour of the gardens on Tuesday? Or the implacable, determined one she'd known in college? Or were they somehow the same? That seemed so unlikely. So, which Duncan was the real one?

Anna slid beneath the bubbles so only her head was above the steaming water. There was nothing like a good soak to get rid of the dirt, grime, and sore back that working in the garden brought with it. She'd finished the first side of the formal garden and not tagged even a single plant. There'd been one brief moment when she thought she'd found a rosebush, but it had turned out to be a stick with a thorny vine wrapped around it. At least she'd checked to be sure before calling Duncan to point it out. Wouldn't he have had just the best time laughing about that one?

She frowned. That was probably unfair. He hadn't done anything to make her think that—not since she'd been at Peacock Hill. And, if she was honest, he hadn't really even in college. He'd just been so sure his choices were the right ones that everyone in their group had gone along with it. And she hadn't been able to present a compelling enough argument for them to do otherwise. That was lowering.

She'd spent plenty of time since then working on her presentation skills. And her confidence. So why was she hiding in a bathtub?

Getting clean wasn't hiding. Everyone needed to be clean after a day in the garden. She'd go down when she was done, get a slice of pizza, shake some hands, and head back up to her room. Then she'd have checked the friendly box and still have time to herself to do...something. There had to be something worth doing in her room.

With a sigh she sank under the bubbles. She loved the echoey quality of all the sounds when you were under water. And the iridescent glamour on the world outside left by the dissipating bubbles gave enough of a shadow that she could, at least for a moment, pretend she was anywhere she wanted to imagine. Anna broke through the water and wiped it from her face.

Someone banged on the door. "Anna?"

She crossed her arms over her chest. Not that anyone could see in. But still. "Yeah?"

"The pizza's gonna be here in about ten. You're coming down, right?"

Ten minutes. The water wouldn't even be cold yet. "Probably. Don't wait for me though, okay?"

"'K. If I don't see you in twenty though, I'm coming back up to drag you down. You'll have fun. Promise."

Anna shook her head. Like Deidre could promise that. Still...pizza...her stomach rumbled. It beat the peanut butter and jelly she'd been living on since she arrived. Why had she thought there'd be a cook? Deidre and Duncan seemed to eat whenever it struck their fancy—which was fine. She operated that way as well. But the kitchen hardly ever looked used when she was in there fixing herself something. She pulled the plug, smiling as the water started to glug down the drain. A quick shower to rinse off all the bubbles and she'd be good enough.

Fifteen minutes later, dressed in faded jeans and a Virginia Tech t-shirt, she took a deep breath and headed downstairs. She followed the laughter into the formal dining room. The room ran from the front to the back of the house and was covered in rich wood paneling. The top molding was ornately carved and the coffered ceiling was incredible. She'd thought a room completely covered in wood—from the parquet floors up—would be dark and unwelcoming. But this space couldn't help looking posh.

The two folding tables set up in the middle of the room looked out of place. As did the mismatched collection of chairs. Deidre was snuggled up against a tall man. She had a plate of pizza on her lap, as did he. When she spotted Anna, she jumped up, nearly dropping her slice on the floor, and clapped her hands.

"You made it!" Deidre set her plate on her seat and crossed to where Anna hovered in the doorway. "Everyone, this is Anna Hamilton. She's helping Duncan with the grounds."

"Hi." Anna lifted a hand and fought the urge to turn and run.

Duncan grinned and brought over a paper plate. "Grab some pizza and find a seat. There are some sodas in the cooler."

She took the plate. "Thanks."

Deidre shot her brother a look before taking Anna's elbow and steering her toward the tables. Two men stood in front of the pizza boxes debating the relative merits of sausage versus mushrooms. "Danny, Matt, this is Anna."

"Hi, Anna. I'm Matt." The slightly taller blond man extended his hand. "Good to meet you."

"You too." She took his hand and shook it before turning to the other man and offering her hand. "Which makes you Danny."

"So they tell me." Danny grinned and took her hand. "I take it you already know Duncan?"

"We went to school together." Duncan reached around Anna for a slice of pizza.

Anna frowned. The move seemed calculated. Territorial. Which was ridiculous. He'd never had any interest in her as anything more than a useful member of a project. "For whatever reason, we ended up on a lot of teams together."

"Interesting." Matt cocked his head to the side. "And now you're here."

"That's Deidre's doing." Anna smiled and reached for a piece of pizza that didn't look like it had too many toppings on it. Did no one like plain cheese anymore?

"Ooo, burn, man." Danny punched Duncan's shoulder.

Duncan offered a tight smile. "No kidding. Maybe I'll go see what's in the cooler."

What had just happened? Anna watched Duncan walk off. "So, Danny. What do you do?"

It was after eleven when Anna dragged herself to her room. That had been fun. There was no other word for it. Deidre was a lucky girl, landing someone like Jeremiah. And even Duncan had been mostly pleasant. After they'd eaten, Deidre had pulled out a pile of board games. Who knew choosing a game to play could be a blast? But it had been. Everyone had such varied opinions and reasons for their choices. In the end, they'd settled on a game that was a cross between telephone and drawing something for others to guess.

It. Was. Hilarious.

For a little while, it had seemed like Matt might have been trying to get to know her in a slightly more than friendly way. Until Duncan scowls from across the room had become almost palpable. What was Duncan's problem, anyway?

Didn't matter. That was a worry for another day. For now, Anna was satisfied with a good week of work under her belt and a fun Friday evening—the first in quite a while. Maybe, just maybe, she'd join them tomorrow night, too.

4

Duncan paced in the foyer. What was Deidre thinking? Inviting Anna to share a meal and hang out on the weekend was one thing, but to church, too? And okay, that sounded backward. But still...did his sister not understand what this was doing to him?

"I didn't keep you waiting, did I?" Anna hurried across the foyer clutching a Bible to her chest.

Duncan shook his head. "You're fine. Deidre caught a ride with Jeremiah—she's used to him picking her up, despite the fact that I'm here. That's okay, right?"

Anna shrugged. "Why wouldn't it be?"

Right. Why wouldn't it be? She clearly didn't feel any of the sparks that he did. Just being in her presence had him on edge—but not in a bad way. He gave a curt nod. "Let's go then."

He held the front door open for her and checked that it locked before heading down to his car, clicking the unlock button as he went. Anna tugged open the passenger door and slid in before he was all the way there. Which was fine. This wasn't a date, so why should he get her door? Still, it rankled. Did she think he didn't know how to be a gentleman?

"How far is it?" Anna clicked her seatbelt into place and gave the strap a tug.

"Not far. It's in town."

"Oh. I expected it to be in Waynesboro. I could've driven and met you there."

Duncan pulled around the stand of cedars and turned down the long driveway that would take them to the road. "Seems a waste when we're going to the same place."

"Yes, but...never mind."

Duncan shook his head. She'd probably been about to list the same objections he'd made about this plan in the first place. Why couldn't Deidre have told Jeremiah she'd meet him there and come with them? Or Jeremiah could've waited and they could've all gone in his truck. Something that didn't leave him and Anna in the same car surrounded by awkward silence.

She cleared her throat. "So. What's it like working at Marshall Brothers?"

How was he supposed to answer that? Maybe honesty was the best policy. "I loved it. Until recently."

"You mentioned that. Management changeovers, I think you said? Before that, then?"

Duncan glanced over. She'd turned in her seat and was looking at him earnestly. "About like any other landscaping firm, I imagine. You're not full-time at the archives, right? So it was probably about like what you've been up to. Helping clients realize the potential of their green spaces—and steering them away from the inevitable bad ideas they come in with."

"So, the final project our senior year was a good representation of what it's like?"

Why was she asking this? "Don't you think it was? My first—oh, I don't know, ten?—clients were all a lot like that project."

"I don't—I'm not..." Anna sighed. "I've never managed to land a corporate job. I've done some independent ones. I even tried to make a go of my own business for a while. Then the archives job came open and the idea of a steady paycheck won out."

Duncan frowned. "And do you like it?"

"It's okay. But not so amazing that I had to think for more than ten seconds when your sister offered me the chance to come help on this. I mean, seriously, having Peacock Hill in my portfolio? That's *got* to be something the Richmond firms would take a second look at."

"More than likely. How long's your vacation?"

"Vacation?"

"Well, we'll want to be sure you get enough for that portfolio before you have to head back to the archives...right?" Duncan shot her a quick smile before he turned into the parking lot at the church.

"I didn't have any vacation to use. I took unpaid leave to come out here."

Questions circled in his brain all through the service. Where was Anna keeping her stuff? What was she living on? Deidre wasn't paying her, was she? The last one, at least, he was going to find out. His sister didn't need to pay someone to help with the landscaping when he was perfectly capable of doing it all without taking a cent.

Deidre poked him with her elbow. She leaned over and whispered in his ear. "I can hear you thinking from over here. What's wrong?"

He shook his head. Now wasn't the time. He'd ask when Anna wasn't sitting on his other side, trying desperately not to look like she was listening in.

The organ started playing and conversations began to bubble around them.

"Seriously, Duncan, what's eating at you?" Deidre frowned at him. "You've been stewing since you sat down. I think your scowl during the greeting time might have scared Mrs. Patterson. And she's not someone you want on your bad side."

Jeremiah grinned as he leaned around Deidre. "It's true. She's already let everyone know your sister snorts when she laughs. Apparently, this is a major negative as far as Mrs. P is concerned. Now that you're a scowler, well, your whole family might just be deemed unfit."

Deidre chuckled and slapped Jeremiah's knee. "It's not that bad. But still. You okay?"

Duncan nodded. "I'm fine."

"If you say so." Shaking her head, Deidre shifted and looked at Jeremiah. "We're having lunch at your parents' again, right?"

"Yup. Duncan and Anna are welcome, too. Obviously."

"Oh. I couldn't impose." Anna's eyes were wide. "I didn't—"

"Nonsense. That's one of the reasons I wanted to make sure you caught a ride—so you couldn't run off and miss out on Mrs. Crawford's cooking." Deidre grinned and stood. "You can follow Jeremiah. I'll make sure he drives like a normal person instead of the lead car in a funeral procession."

Anna didn't say anything, but she didn't look happy.

Duncan didn't blame her. Not that he had anything more pressing on her plan for the day. Deidre was adamant that they not work on Sunday—he wouldn't have anyway—but that didn't mean he needed to spend the day schmoozing with people he didn't know. But looking at his sister as she walked hand-in-hand with Jeremiah...he wasn't going to talk her out of it.

"Come on. We'll go, eat, and leave as soon as it's polite to do so. Deal?"

Anna nodded. "All right."

Duncan's smile was tight as he opened the door for Anna. Should he just ask? He rounded the car and slid behind the wheel. "How are you able to take a month of unpaid leave?"

Anna sighed. "Savings? I don't have a lot of expenses and the library pays okay. My parents bought my car when I graduated from college, so it's rent, gas, and food. I've been tucking away everything else. I'd been planning to take six months and see the world. And I might still. But this opportunity seemed worth putting a little dent in that timeline."

Huh. That was some saving. He socked a little away each paycheck but he still wouldn't have been comfortable with a month off unpaid. She was brave. And it said a lot about who she was. "I'm impressed."

"Thanks." She offered a tiny smile before turning to look out the passenger window. Duncan might not be a pro at reading women, but he could tell when a conversation was over.

The Crawfords didn't live far from the church. Following Jeremiah was no problem—he was conscientious. Deidre had told Duncan about the first time she followed Jeremiah, when he'd driven like an eighty-year-old woman. At least she'd been able to get him to drive at normal speeds. He parked behind Jeremiah's truck and cut off the engine. The Crawfords' house was a two-story, stone-faced home with a porch that looked like it wrapped around to the back. The front yard was probably the same as it'd been when the developer finished with it in the late 1960s. There was so much potential for it to be great, though.

In his mind, Duncan sketched out a better path from the street to the front door—one that connected to the driveway and garage and made little planting areas to break up the sea of grass.

Anna caught up to him as he started up the sidewalk. "The porch needs planters. Boxes on the rail and something big on either side of the door."

He chuckled. "Thank goodness it's not just me. I was redesigning this path and making new beds—that stand of birch trees is crying for some shade plants to go under it."

"It is. What sort of path were you thinking?"

"Maybe brick pavers in a herringbone? Something that would set off the house rather than detract from it. The stone is so distinctive, this concrete...it's not good."

"What's not good?" Deidre stood on the front porch waiting for them.

Heat burned up Duncan's neck. "Nothing. Occupational hazard."

"Ah. You're redesigning their yard." Deidre grinned. "I do that with people's houses. You'll like the back. It's better. In fact, Jeremiah's been talking to them about a waterfall his mom wants. Maybe you'll have some ideas."

"Hey." Jeremiah pushed open the screen door. "Don't be giving away my business. These are some of my best customers."

Duncan smiled. "I can consult, if you need any help."

"I might take you up on that. Mom always has ideas. Come on in. My folks are out back."

Duncan gestured for Anna to go ahead of him. Something smelled good. Fresh biscuits? His stomach rumbled. The one thing he hadn't thought through as clearly as he should have before coming down was the food situation. Neither he nor his sister was particularly adept in the kitchen. Oh, they wouldn't starve, but starvation was a far cry from eating well. And so far, Anna hadn't been much of an improvement in that department. In fact, she seemed to eat at odd hours— he'd only run into her in the kitchen once. Maybe that was by design?

He followed the group through the house and out into the back yard. Deidre was right, the back was much nicer. "You're not going to put the water feature in that back corner, are you?"

"Actually, that's exactly where Mom was thinking it should go." Jeremiah frowned. "Why?"

"Oh. There's nothing wrong with that." Duncan tucked his hands in his pockets and deliberately turned away from the cliché corner. He could find four better places just scanning the yard. Except that you did what the client wanted.

"But?" Jeremiah moved to stand next to Duncan and look out over the yard.

Duncan sighed. "It's kind of obvious. And I've always thought waterfalls should be unexpected. So you stumble over them and get hit with that little rush of delight."

"Oh, that's just how waterfalls should be." Duncan turned as Mrs. Crawford set a platter of hamburger fixings—buns, tomato slices, lettuce, and a jumble of sauces and spreads in little glass bowls—on the table. "Have you been hiking off Skyline Drive? That's how I always feel when we get to one of the falls. Even when we know it's there."

"I haven't, no." Duncan smiled. "I'll make a point to do that while I'm down here."

Mrs. Crawford smiled. "How are those burgers coming, honey?"

Mr. Crawford opened the grill and peeked in. "They're ready when you are. Did you bring the biscuits?"

"I'll go get them, Dad." Jeremiah patted his mother's shoulder as he passed her.

"Honestly. Who puts a hamburger on a biscuit?" Mrs. Crawford shook her head as she pulled a chair out from the patio table. "Don't be shy now. Everyone grab a plate and seat."

Anna poked Duncan in the side with her elbow as she passed him.

"What was that for?" Duncan trailed after her, the idea of a hamburger on a biscuit still turning over in his mind. He might just try that. The biscuits had smelled heavenly.

"Getting all waterfall snobby on them. There's nothing wrong with that corner." Anna plopped into a chair and reached for the stack of paper plates.

"I said that. But you have to admit there are better places." He took a plate off the top of the stack when Anna passed them to him.

Anna shrugged. "Client is king."

He'd said that, too. At least in his mind. But whatever. The Crawfords weren't *his* clients, they were Jeremiah's clients. And parents. Duncan wasn't looking to start a landscaping business. He'd help his sister get Peacock Hill running, find her a full-time grounds keeper, and then go back to D.C.

His gut twisted.

Jeremiah came back out and set a plate of biscuits on the table before claiming the seat by Deidre and brushing a kiss across her cheek. "Regardless of what my mom says, if you're even remotely curious about the biscuit burger thing, you need to try it. You might never go back. Although, Mom's biscuits are better than any other I've tried."

"That's 'cause her secret ingredient is love." Mr. Crawford set the plate of grilled patties on the crowded table and sat next to his wife.

Mrs. Crawford made a shooing motion with her hand. "Flatterers. Both of you. They're just my grandma's biscuits and I'll happily provide the recipe to whoever wants it. Now, why doesn't Jeremiah say a blessing and we'll eat?"

Jeremiah took Deidre's hand and bowed his head. Duncan closed his eyes, clenching his teeth at the stab in his heart that came from seeing his sister so clearly in love. It was a good thing. Jeremiah seemed like a great guy. But...Duncan was older and had always imagined he'd find someone for himself long before his little sister had bridal bouquets and stars in her eyes.

Anna nudged his side.

Duncan's eyes flew open and he turned to glare at her. "What is your problem?"

"You okay, Duncan?" Deidre's eyebrows were practically in her hairline.

Duncan made a show of scooting away from Anna. "Apparently I'm sitting too close to Anna's elbows."

Everyone around the table—with the notable exception of Anna—chuckled, and conversation picked up.

"I was trying to let you know the prayer had ended." Anna shot him a saccharine smile and reached for a bun. "My apologies."

Duncan took a biscuit and sliced it in half. "I appreciate the thought, though my ribs could have handled a gentler messenger."

"Poor baby." Anna rolled her eyes and dropped a tomato slice on top of her hamburger. "Are you going to tell them where to put the water feature?"

Duncan shook his head. It really wasn't his business.

"Oh! Is that why you were talking about waterfalls?" Mrs. Crawford beamed and set her burger back on her plate. "Jeremiah hasn't had a lot of time to devote to the idea yet. I forgot we had a professional in town now."

"Hey." Jeremiah waved his hand and quickly chewed and swallowed. "As it's part of what I do for a living, I am, in fact, a professional."

Deidre patted Jeremiah's arm.

Anna snickered.

"If looking around your back yard is any indication, he does wonderful work. You're in good hands." Duncan took a huge bite from his burger and tried not to cough. The biscuit was quite a bit drier than a bun. He should have added some mayo or ketchup or...something. But at least it would keep him from being able to talk.

"Let me get you some iced tea." Mrs. Crawford poured a cup and passed it to Duncan. "Now, I know my son is great at what he does. But what he loves is the handyman thing—building and fixing structures. The lawn care is what he does to build up a cushion against the winter when projects drop off. And so what he usually does is exactly what I ask him to do—maybe with a few little tweaks if he gets interested in the project. Right, Jeremiah?"

Jeremiah hunched his shoulders at his mother's arch look. "Yes, ma'am."

Mrs. Crawford nodded and, with a smile, turned back to Duncan. "Which is why I just *know* he isn't going to mind if you give him some tips about the fountain."

Duncan took a sip of tea and continued to chew. How could he get out of this conversation gracefully?

"Of course. Tips are always good." Jeremiah grabbed the bag of chips from the middle of the table and shook some onto his plate. "Like where to put it. You were saying something about that back corner not being a great spot?"

"What's wrong with the back corner?" Mrs. Crawford frowned at Duncan. "Sybil Hollands, our neighbor two doors down, has a waterfall in the back corner of her yard and it's lovely."

Duncan swallowed his bite, but it did nothing for the lump lodged in his throat. He took another drink. "I think I said there was nothing wrong with that corner. It's just...expected. And I've always thought it was more fun to put things where they're a bit more of a surprise."

"Nicely done." Mr. Crawford beamed at Duncan before pointing a finger at his wife. "As are the biscuits, hon. Now, since I'm sure Jeremiah and Duncan can put their heads together about my back yard later, when the rest of us won't be bored to tears, why doesn't Deidre tell us about the progress she's making on Peacock Hill and when you're going to let us all come up there to see it?"

Deidre laughed and began to talk about her plaster repair in the breakfast room and her hopes of finding a painter who could replicate the tromp l'oeil that adorned the walls previously.

Duncan mouthed "sorry" to Jeremiah, who shrugged. At least the guy didn't seem too bent out of shape. One of these days, Duncan was going to have to learn to think before he opened his mouth.

5

Anna planted her hands on her hips and surveyed the ground where the formal garden would go. She'd put in two days with the compact excavator clearing out all the old plants until all that remained was dirt. Now there was a blank slate and she was itching to get started.

"That looks so much better." Deidre climbed the last of the stone stairs that led to the garden from the driveway behind the mansion. "What's next?"

"I guess that depends. Do you want to recreate what they had in the early nineteen hundreds? Or did you want to put your own stamp on things?"

"Hmm. I hadn't really considered doing anything other than restoration. I wouldn't want anything modern—"

"Oh gosh, no. I just meant reworking where the paths go. Using different plants. That kind of thing. And, to be honest, the plants are mostly guesses from the photos. But some are obvious."

"Ah." Deidre's gaze slid to meet Anna's. "Have you talked to my brother?"

Duncan. No, she'd been doing her very best to avoid just that. "It's your house."

"And he knows that I don't have a clue about gardens and landscapes. I just want it to look nice and be something that could have been here when the house was in its heyday. Beyond that?" Deidre shrugged. "I'm hopeless if we're talking about more than cutting grass."

"Right." Anna blew out a breath. "I guess I need to find Duncan and talk to him. Any idea if it's better to go in prepared with options? Or is that going to step on his toes?"

"Whatever you think is easiest. He's not territorial. Or hard to work with." Deidre paused. "Or, at least, I've never found him to be that way."

Right. 'Cause Deidre was his sister. And probably never had to fight to be heard in a roomful of guys who all thought they knew better than the weirdo girl who wanted to do landscaping. Although...if she was honest, Duncan had never led the charge to talk over her. Even if he never did anything to stop it—like taking her ideas. "All right."

"He's working in the left side garden, if you want to find him."

Anna shook her head. "Not yet. I'll go put something together."

"He might already have a plan."

She blew out a breath. Of course he did. "You're right. Left side?"

Deidre pointed.

"'K. Thanks." Anna trudged across the grassy space that ran between the two garden areas before heading down the far steps toward where Duncan was working. Gravel crunched under her feet as she crossed the driveway. Why had she stayed when she realized this wouldn't be her project? Was she going to be anything more than a grunt? That wasn't the kind of experience her resume needed. Anyone could put something in the ground and water it. She wanted to design the space and make it beautiful. To have her mark on something that, down the road, might be recognized as hers.

She reached the top of the stairs that led to the sunken garden on the left side of the house and paused, her breath catching in her lungs. He had his shirt off and his muscles rippled as he used a flat-edged shovel to pry up one of the marble paving stones that made the floor. There was a stack of the stones leaning against the far garden wall—it looked like he was about half-way through. If he planned to remove them all.

Anna licked her lips and pulled her thoughts back to her errand. "Duncan?"

He looked up and dragged his arm across his forehead. "Hey. It looks great up there. No more wild, tangled mess."

"Thanks." What time had he gotten up? She'd been up there since a little after seven doing a final sweep. It wasn't quite ten. "I was wondering what you thought the next step should be."

Duncan squatted to pick up the paver and carry it to the wall. He set it with the others and brushed his hands on his jeans, leaving streaks of soil behind. "Depends, I guess. Do you think we should recreate exactly what was there—or as exactly as we can? Or should we take the general idea and modernize it some?"

Anna laughed and sat on the top step. "Those were my questions. Deidre said to talk to you."

He grabbed the t-shirt he'd discarded and tugged it over his head. Anna fought a frown. Which was ridiculous. She wasn't here to ogle the man. Even if he was supremely prime. He'd had a good build in college, but his years working had honed and defined it. It was obvious he didn't spend all his time behind a desk in D.C.

"You in there?" Duncan nudged her with his elbow.

He was sitting next to her, chugging from a water bottle. And she'd spaced out thinking about his body. Heat flooded her face. This was worse than college. "Yeah. Sorry. So—the formal gardens?"

"I'd like to hear your thoughts. I know we need to stay in the style, but do you have any idea about specifics?"

She had ideas. Too many of them. And sitting this close to Duncan, not all of them were about the garden. She was a fool. Anna cleared her throat. "Um. I can put some together. I was thinking it might be fun to take the general idea and modernize it a little. People don't really stroll in the gardens for entertainment anymore, you know?"

Duncan nodded.

"So, we need to do something that makes that an interesting idea. What's your sister's plan for this place when it's all done?"

"Weddings and small retreats or conferences. Why?"

"Hmm. With weddings, you'll want to have good places for photos. And an outdoor venue, right?"

"I figured the arbor would serve for a venue. But photos...having a garden set up that facilitates different styles of portraits would be good."

The arbor would, once it was fixed up, be a great venue for a larger wedding. But a more intimate one would get lost. "What about smaller weddings?"

"What do you mean?"

"The arbor and the lawn are huge. They're going to overwhelm anything that's fewer than fifty people. We could make one side a more open formal garden—give it high hedge walls so it feels private but room inside for twenty or thirty chairs in rows. Some kind of focal point at one end that would serve for the ceremony?" Anna's fingers itched for a pencil and paper. She could see it. Could he?

Duncan pursed his lips before nodding slowly. "That could work. The other side wouldn't mirror it?"

Anna shook her head. That was a departure from what was traditional, but it made more sense for this use. "We could design the other side with meandering paths and nooks—some with benches—for pictures. Or just wandering."

"I like that idea. I like it a lot. Can you draw it up and we'll run it by Deidre?"

She nodded. "Do you think she'll like it?"

"I can't see why she wouldn't. It's a great idea."

Anna grinned, her whole body warming under his approving look. "Okay. I'll go put some sketches together. I can probably have something ready by one—maybe you can talk her into a late lunch and we could go over them?"

Duncan hesitated briefly before nodding. "That sounds good."

What was she doing? Anna stood and brushed off the back of her jeans, overwhelmingly aware that what she really wanted was to have lunch with Duncan. Alone. And not to talk about gardens, either. How was it possible that, in ten days, she'd gone from being completely over her college crush to more hung up on the guy than ever before?

Her palms were sweating. This was worse than any project in school. Was it because it had been so long since she'd done any kind of client presentation? At the archives, she fulfilled requests for information. It wasn't her work on the line—or her ideas. She spent time researching, that was it, and she got paid even if it wasn't what the person was looking for. Presenting that information was still a presentation. Kind of. This one though...if Deidre hated it, would she send her away?

Anna took a deep breath and let it out through tight lips. Duncan had liked the idea. Deidre seemed like she was willing—happy, even—to be guided by him. So maybe it'd be okay. She flipped through the printouts from the landscape design software she had on her laptop, thanking God that she'd gone ahead and thrown the small printer in her car after all. Her hand-drawn designs weren't bad, but they lacked the professionalism the computer gave. Of course, they weren't as colorful as her drawings. She pulled her lower lip between her teeth. She'd go ahead and take those, too. There was no rule saying she had to show them.

Armed with her designs and a churning belly, Anna headed down to the kitchen. Duncan had texted her to let her know he and Deidre would meet her there. Laughter met her at the door and some of the tightness in her muscles eased. At least it sounded like Deidre was in a good mood. Not that she'd ever encountered the woman in any other kind of mood. She pushed open the door and stopped. Jeremiah sat beside Deidre at the small table on the far wall. Their heads were together and Anna could practically see little cartoon hearts around them. Duncan was nowhere to be seen.

Anna cleared her throat.

"Hey." Deidre looked over but didn't move away from Jeremiah. "If you want to make yourself some lunch, go for it. Or I can make you a sandwich? Duncan said he'd be another couple of minutes. You don't mind if Jeremiah joins us, do you?"

"No, of course not." Anna forced a smile. What a lie. She'd be happier if she could just drop the drawings and run. And this was one of the reasons her job interviews always went so poorly. People skills. She had them—when she had to—but they came at a big expense. Plants and dirt were so much easier. "I'm not really hungry."

Deidre opened her mouth and snapped it shut. "Suit yourself. Have a seat."

Anna crossed to the table and pulled out a chair. She sat, set her papers on the table, and folded her hands over them. "How's the renovating going?"

Jeremiah laughed. "Are you sure you want to start that conversation? I'm in the business and still sometimes zone out if she gets going with details."

"You're a riot." Deidre bumped his shoulder with her own before smiling at Anna. "It's going well. I finished sanding the last of the plaster fixes in the breakfast room this morning. So it's ready to repaint. I'm trying to decide if I need to get everything on this floor, at least, back together first and then paint, or if I can do it one room at a time."

Anna nodded. "Pros and cons of both, I imagine?"

"Yeah."

Jeremiah shook his head. "I don't think so. It's better to get everything else fixed up and then do a big painting extravaganza. That way you don't get dust or whatever in your drying paint when it wafts over from sanding plaster in the music room. And honestly? I think you probably ought to get the whole house ready before you paint, not just this floor."

Deidre groaned. "You're probably right, but I want to have a finished room."

Anna smiled. That was a feeling she understood. Sometimes it was a pain to put in the smaller, more affordable plants knowing that she wasn't likely to ever see the full effect of maturity. "How long will that be, do you think?"

"Claire, our sister, is planning to move down this weekend. She's a whiz at tile. I'll get her going on the bathrooms. Realistically though? Another six months. At least."

Duncan pushed through the kitchen door. "Sorry I'm late. I was sure I'd be able to get that fish fountain working, but I still haven't found the leaking pipe. I may end up digging it all up and re-plumbing it."

"Bummer. You want some food? I can fix you a sandwich." Deidre pointed to the last chair. "You should sit. You look beat."

Duncan dropped into the chair. He was filthy. There were obvious signs that he'd tried to brush off the bulk of the soil and mud, but it was just as clear that he'd been lying in the dirt. "I wouldn't say no if there's still some pastrami in there."

Deidre hopped off her chair and crossed to the fridge. "You can start if you want, Anna."

"I don't mind waiting." It couldn't take that long to build a sandwich, could it? And then Deidre could see the design instead of having to imagine it.

Duncan flashed a grin. "My sister doesn't understand how landscape presentations work, obviously.

Anna's been up there making drawings. If they're still as good as the ones she did in college, you don't want to miss them."

Anna's cheeks burned and she glanced down at the papers on the table. He'd never complimented her work in school. Not to her, at least. Though she had always ended up with the drawing tasks on their group projects. Was it because he thought she had talent? She'd always assumed it was because he hadn't thought she was able to handle anything more. What else had she misread?

Deidre slid a plate with an enormous sandwich on it and a bottle of water in front of Duncan. "Okay. I'm ready."

The butterflies in her stomach that had finally settled leapt back into their aerial antics. Anna cleared her throat. "Okay. So, talking with Duncan, he said you were thinking of a wedding, conference, and retreat venue?"

Deidre nodded.

"Right. Weddings, in particular, would probably want to use the gardens. Or at least to have the option. I mean, I could see making a grand entrance as a bride on that staircase with the stained-glass window behind me, but that might not be for everyone." Anna took a deep breath and, with shaking hands, flipped over the first picture. She gave herself a mental kick to try and stop the rambling before continuing. "With a larger wedding, the lawn and arbor make a great venue. The arbor needs to be cleaned up and planted—I was thinking wisteria for some color—and then three fairly large urns down each side of the grass. I'd plant them with some basic greenery so that brides could then tuck in their own arrangements and bring in their colors."

Deidre slid the drawing closer and traced her fingers over the scrollwork on the planter option Anna had included. "I like this. But what about the side gardens? Isn't that what you were asking about?"

Mouth full, Duncan pointed at Deidre.

"Sorry. I get caught up." Deidre raised her hands. "Go on."

"Okay, so that works well for big weddings, but if someone had fewer than fifty, they're going to get lost on that lawn. So, I was thinking..." She took another calming breath and turned over the next drawing. "One of the side gardens could go this route. It's more open, basically a big rectangle inside a privacy hedge. Traditionally, there would be paths along the outside and plantings down the middle. Probably a fountain. But to make it more wedding-friendly, I went with beds along the bottom of the hedges."

"I like this." Deidre smiled and pulled the printout closer. "Are these urns the same?"

Anna nodded. "I thought it would be good to keep them consistent...but I have other options you can look at."

"Maybe the same general design, but taller and slimmer?" Duncan spun the page a little to squint at it. "The smaller space might get overwhelmed by the larger ones."

"I'd wondered about that." Anna slid another page to Duncan. "So I did look these up. Same general style but, like you said, taller and slimmer. It makes it more challenging to get the brides' own arrangements worked in, but still doable."

"Nice." Duncan pushed that piece of paper to Deidre, whose eyes lit up.

"Oh. That's gorgeous. Do you know what flowers those would be, or were you doodling?"

"I know. But it's just an example of how a bridal floral arrangement might fit in." Anna scrunched her forehead. "I wasn't thinking of it being permanent."

"No. I get that. It's just..." Deidre's gaze slid to Jeremiah. "I'll talk to you about it later. So far I'm sold. What about the other side? I don't think we need three wedding venues, especially since that'd be the same size as this smaller one, right?"

Anna chuckled and flipped over the last of the printouts. "For the other side, I was thinking more like a—well, almost a maze—with nooks here and there for photos."

Deidre studied the paper for several seconds before looking up. "You can do this?"

Duncan slid it across the table and looked at it, nodding.

"I think so." Anna clasped her hands together.

"You can. Absolutely. And I want to help. This is unique and cool but still would fit perfectly in to Peacock Hill." Duncan held her gaze. "Nice job. Really nice job."

Anna looked away, her cheeks burning and her heart thudding in her chest. The complement was potent. But not nearly as intoxicating as him.

Jeremiah wiggled his fingers. "Can I see?"

"Nope." Deidre laughed and passed him the sheets. "What do you think?"

"I'm impressed." Jeremiah grinned and nodded toward the other papers that Anna hadn't flipped. "What are those?"

"Oh. Um. Just my drawings. The printouts give you a more professional..." She broke off when Duncan wiggled the pages out from under her arms and spread them out on the table. The riot of colors seemed to leap off the page. Her fingers itched to snatch the papers back. "I didn't..."

"These are great." Deidre moved them around. "We should frame them and put them in the hallway or something. Give people a sense of the thought that goes into a project like this."

"Oh, no. They're not—they're just sketches." Anna reached for them, her cheeks on fire. "I'm not sure why I brought them with me."

"Because you're talented. And if you hadn't sold her with your presentation and the computer-based designs, I bet these would've turned the tide." Duncan laid his hand on hers.

Anna froze as shivers tingled up her arm and spine. Her mouth was dry. "Okay. Um. So, Deidre, you like that idea?"

"I really do."

"Then I'll get started on a plan and prices and that sort of thing. I'll need to do more clearing. If I can use the excavator tomorrow, I can get that done and maybe start putting things in next week, depending on suppliers." Anna nodded and stood, her chair crashing to the floor. "So. Bye."

She fled the room, her system still buzzing from Duncan's touch. She might have a plan for the garden, but now she desperately needed one that would keep her heart whole.

6

Duncan grabbed two cans of soda from the fridge. It was almost eleven. Surely that meant it was time for a break. Anna had sunk her teeth into her part of the garden project and he'd barely seen her for the last two days. But if he let himself, he could still feel her hand under his. What would it be like to have her wind their fingers together and sit close to him so their bodies nearly touched the way Deidre and Jeremiah did? He'd wondered those things—or variations thereof—off and on since college. Maybe it was time to find out.

He stepped out the back door onto the porte cocheré. The enormous marble fountain greeted him. It was practically begging to be put to rights. But the side gardens came first. They were ostensibly the easier project. Not that it had gone as smoothly as he'd hoped. With a last look at the forlorn lion's head, he angled up the stairs to the gardens where Anna was working.

She stood with her hands planted on her hips. The sunlight hit her hair, turning some strands into a lighter, honeyed brown.

"Hey. I brought you a soda." Duncan held out one of the cans and came to stand beside her. "It's looking good."

Anna gave a short laugh and took the drink, popping the tab. "It's a start, at least. Thanks for this."

He nodded as she tipped her head back and took a long drink. He shouldn't stare. And watching someone hydrate shouldn't make his insides quiver. Duncan cleared his throat. "I was wondering if you have plans tonight."

"Isn't your other sister—Claire, right?—showing up tonight? Figured there'd be pizza or something."

How had he forgotten Claire arrived tonight? And she was bringing her stuff in a big truck. It was probably bad form to be gone when she arrived. And yet... "Right. She'll probably be tired. I hadn't asked Deidre what she had planned. But, um, if there isn't pizza and a 'welcome home' Claire thing, do you maybe want to grab dinner? We could head over to Waynesboro."

Anna's eyes widened. "I...I'm not sure I understand."

Duncan took a deep breath. "A date. I'm asking you out on a date. If that's out of line, I apologize."

"Oh. Why?"

How was he supposed to answer that question? "I thought...you know what, never mind."

"Duncan, wait."

"Yeah?"

"I'm sorry. I'd like that."

"You're sure?"

Anna nodded.

Muscles he hadn't realized were tight loosened. He could welcome Claire anytime. "Great. Plan to leave around five?"

"Okay. I'll meet you in the front hall."

He grinned. "Perfect."

Anna finished the soda and offered the empty can. "Will you take this? I don't want to forget it when it's time to go back in."

"Sure." Duncan took the can. "See you tonight."

"Okay."

Whistling, Duncan headed back down toward the house. He set Anna's empty can, and his untouched one, on the steps by the back door, and went around to the sunken garden. *Why.* Who asked why when someone asked them on a date? That was a puzzler, for sure. But she'd said yes. And that was something to be thankful for. Now he just had to come up with an outing that would leave her willing to do it again.

"This is nicer than I expected." Anna glanced around the quiet lobby of the restaurant, done in shades of brown and gold, and brushed at her dark jeans. The occasional laugh and clink of a fork on a plate wafted from the dining room through the door to their right.

"You look great." Duncan smiled and checked himself in the middle of reaching for her hand. She might want reassurance about her outfit, but at this point, she hadn't given him any indication that he could touch her again. And he'd been watching for one.

A willowy blonde slipped through the door and went to stand behind the enormous wooden podium. "May I help you?"

"McIntyre? We have a six o'clock reservation."

The woman consulted a fat leather book and nodded. "This way."

"Reservations?"

Duncan shrugged. "Probably didn't need them, but it seemed like it would be better to have them than not."

Anna gave an absentminded nod and followed the hostess. What was going through her head? Was this too much? Too date-like? He'd said it was a date...should he have clarified that he hadn't meant just as friends? Duncan sighed and slid into the tall booth opposite Anna.

The table in front of them contained an inset heating element. The hostess spun the dial at the corner of the metal plate surrounding it before offering them menus. "Someone will be right with you. Enjoy."

Anna looked at the menu for a moment before setting it in front of her and folding her arms on top of it. "Why are we here, Duncan?"

She probably wasn't asking from an existential standpoint. Duncan bit back the default joking reply. Could she really not know? Did he dare to put his cards on the table? What was it Deidre had said? Nothing ventured...he took a deep breath. "Other than to eat dinner?"

Anna's lips thinned. "Other than that."

So much for avoiding the joking reply. "I like you. I basically always have. Since sophomore year, at least. Did you really not know that?"

Her lips parted then closed as she shook her head. "You always acted like you hated me."

"What? When?" She couldn't have said anything that would have surprised him more. He'd spent three years doing everything he could to avoid being obvious about how much he was interested in her. First because she'd had a boyfriend and then, after they'd broken up, out of habit and a sense that he wasn't good enough for her.

"Every time we had to work together?" Anna fidgeted with the menu, straightening it so it was in perfect alignment with the edge of the table. "You never took any of my ideas. It seemed like I always ended up with the grunt jobs."

He swallowed. Maybe their server would show up and save him from having to explain. Or a giant sinkhole could form under his half of the booth. Either would be fine. But there didn't seem to be a rescue coming. "I'm sorry."

Anna arched an eyebrow. "That's it?"

"I'm not sure what else you want. I didn't mean for you to feel that way. But it also seems faintly ridiculous to try and explain myself at this point." He reached up and rubbed the back of his neck. "Knowing you felt that way explains a few things though."

One corner of her mouth lifted. "I imagine it does. I probably owe you an apology too."

"Don't worry about it. It was a long time ago."

"Good evening. Have you dined with us before?"

Duncan barely managed not to laugh when the server appeared. Of course he'd show up now.

Anna shook her head.

"I have. But go ahead and do the spiel." Duncan smiled as the server started in on an explanation of the different fondues available and how they worked.

Anna turned pages in the menu as the man talked, pausing as he leaned over to point to the various options. "It seems more complicated than dinner ought to be."

"If you want something easier, I recommend the meal for two." The server reached over and turned a page in Anna's menu before tapping the top right side. "That way you get to try all three types of fondue. Do you have any questions?"

"We probably need a minute." Duncan waited for Anna to look up and meet his gaze.

She nodded.

"Of course. Can I get you drinks while you look over the options?"

They gave him their choices and he faded out of sight.

"This is awfully expensive. You didn't have—"

"I wanted to. I like the food. I like the fact that it's a good meal for conversation. And it takes a while to eat, which adds a bonus of extra time with you." Duncan picked up his menu and opened it, shielding his face from her gaze. He'd said too much, like he usually did. Which was why he'd never asked her out in college. He probably would've meant to invite her to coffee and ended up proposing instead.

Anna cleared her throat. "So. This thing for two people...does that sound good?"

He flipped to that page and scanned it. "Sure. I like them all, so you can choose, if you'd like."

"Are you sure?"

Duncan nodded and set his menu aside. Maybe asking her out had been a mistake after all. He couldn't control his tongue around her any better now than he'd been able to in college. Though at least now he just sounded stupid. Or desperate. In college he'd apparently been mean.

The server came with their sodas and, with a little back and forth, took their order.

"So." Anna spun her glass between her fingers. "Sophomore year, huh?"

Heat flooded his face but he nodded. "About then, yeah."

"Why didn't you ever say something?"

"Well, there was Marcus for like a year and a half."

She laughed. "Gosh. I'd forgotten about him. And that sounds terrible when we dated for so long."

"A little."

"It's worse than that, honestly. I basically stayed with him because I didn't want to be alone on Friday nights. Not my finest moment." Anna shook her head. "When Marcus figured that out, he dumped me. As he should have. What about after that?"

Duncan took a long drink from his glass.

The server appeared with a pot, which he set on the burner. "I'll get this heating and be back when it starts to steam to prepare your cheese course. Your salads should be out soon."

Maybe it was time to change the subject. "Have you figured out what you need to order for the garden beds?"

Anna frowned. "I didn't bring the list with me, but yes. I thought I'd drive in to Charlottesville on Monday and look around at the garden center your sister mentioned."

"Can I tag along?"

"Of course. Duncan..." Anna trailed off when the server reappeared carrying a tray laden with bowls.

"It'll just take me a minute to get this started." Their server poured some liquid into the bottom of the pot before stirring in shredded cheese and assorted seasonings. "Give this a few minutes, 'til it's bubbly, and then you can dig in. You have bread and assorted vegetables for dippers, make sure not to eat off the fondue forks, they get very hot."

"Can we pray?" Duncan held out a hand.

Anna hesitated for a moment before placing her hand in his. At the touch of her silken skin, shivers worked their way up his arm. He peeked at her through half-closed eyes. Did she feel it at all?

"Jesus, thank you for this food. Please bless it to our bodies. Thank You for Anna and the skill and vision she brings to the garden project. Keep us close to You and in Your will. Amen."

"Amen." Anna took a piece of bread and poked it onto the twin prongs of her fondue fork before swirling it in the bubbling cheese. "I don't think I realized you were a believer before coming to Peacock Hill."

"I'm not surprised. In college I had...I guess you'd call it a crisis of faith. I was away from home and questioning everything I believed. I guess I wanted to make sure I had faith because of my own decisions, not my parents'. If that makes sense?"

"Sure. I think everyone goes through that to some extent. But you never went completely off the rails."

He laughed and dipped bread into the cheese. "No. I didn't want to be someone who I wasn't. Mostly I wanted to sleep in on Sunday mornings without feeling guilty about it."

"Did you ever manage it?"

"Not once." He smiled and popped the cheesy bread in his mouth.

"So what happened?"

"Half-way through the summer between sophomore and junior year I helped out on a week-long mission trip with our church's youth. I guess I had an epiphany of sorts. I'd been waffling because I'd gotten it in my head that believing in Jesus meant I should feel some kind of constant pull in the right direction every minute of every day. But one night, the youth pastor talked about Hebrews eleven verse one, you know about faith being confidence in things hoped for and assurance for what we don't see. Nothing fancy. Simple. And yet difficult. But it clicked and I realized that I had that—so I had faith. My own faith. And it was time to start living like it."

Anna nodded and stabbed the last piece of bread. "What do you need at the garden center?"

"What?"

"Monday? You asked to tag along? What do you need?"

More time with Anna was at the top of his list. Even though their date had gotten off to a rocky start, they seemed to be settling in. "I wanted to poke around their water feature section. Now that I have the one sunken garden fountain working, it should be simple enough to get the other side going. At least, I assume it should. So I thought I'd look and see if I could get any ideas for the big lion head."

"You're really going to try and get that working again?" She smiled, her eyes lighting. "I bet it's beautiful when it's running."

"You don't have pictures?"

"Not that I remember. I'll skim through again when we get back home and double-check."

The server came back with a new pot. He cleared the empty cheese pot and dipping baskets and laid out plates of raw meat. After explaining the cooking times for each item, he disappeared.

"Duncan?"

He slid his two forks into the hot broth and met her gaze. "Yeah?"

"Thanks for asking me out tonight."

He grinned. Maybe this could be the start of something after all. "Thanks for coming."

7

Anna checked her folder for the tenth time that morning. The garden plans were there, as was the list she'd been refining since Friday evening. She smiled, a warm tingle in her belly. Friday night had been so much better than she'd anticipated. Granted, she'd had a strange combination of exceedingly high and terrifyingly low expectations. Somehow, Duncan had managed to avoid the latter and surpass the former. She caught herself before she doodled a heart in the corner of her list. She could hear the questions about it already—from everyone who looked at the thing, most likely. With as easily as she blushed, there'd be no evasion either. She'd made it through their date—and the rest of the weekend— without confessing that she'd had a huge crush on him in college as well. She'd like to keep it that way. Knowing he'd had one on her was a leg up. She probably needed whatever advantages she could find. After all, both of Duncan's sisters lived at Peacock Hill...and they'd probably be happy enough to spy on his behalf.

She clipped the pen to the folder, hooked her purse over her shoulder, and opened her bedroom door. Claire stood in the hall, poised to knock.

"Hey." Claire lowered her hand and grinned. "I heard you're headed into Charlottesville. Can I tag along?"

Anna's heart sank. She'd been looking forward to more time alone with Duncan since he dropped her outside her bedroom door and headed up to the third floor. Between Claire's arrival, Duncan scouting out the lion fountain, and church on Sunday, there hadn't been time for more than a smile across the room. It was interesting to have a group of friends again—and that's what they'd become over the last couple of weeks—but they were also kind of in the way. Still. "Of course. You'll have to fight Duncan for shotgun."

Claire laughed. "I can take him. I know where he's ticklish."

"Great." Anna forced a smile and prayed her face didn't give her away. "I was going to get some coffee and maybe a bite to eat. Thirty minutes?"

"'K. I'll be ready." Claire jogged down the hall to the room she'd claimed and disappeared.

"Perfect." It wasn't quite a mutter, but it was petulant, even to her ears. Maybe this was better. She'd been building up the date with Duncan in her mind since it happened. It was possible he'd been avoiding her all weekend, wasn't it? She frowned and headed down the staircase, barely noticing the stained glass that usually entranced her for a full minute as she descended. What if that was the case? Would he say something? Let her down easy?

Anna turned toward the kitchen and ran straight into something solid.

"Oof." Duncan's voice held laughter around the edges. "Morning. Still half-asleep?"

Heat burned across her cheeks. At least she hadn't dropped her folder and sent papers scattering everywhere. "Apparently. I was heading for coffee."

He pursed his lips and nodded. "I could stand another cup. Can I join you?"

"Sure." Her concern eased. If he'd been avoiding her, he wouldn't follow her to the kitchen when he was clearly on his way from there, would he? This was ridiculous. She needed to relax.

The kitchen was blessedly empty and the coffee pot still half-full. Anna grabbed a mug from the cabinet above the pot and glanced over her shoulder. "New cup?"

"Nah." Duncan reached into the sink and pulled out a blue mug. He ran it under the tap and set it beside the coffee pot. "I'll get the creamer. You like the French vanilla one, right?"

Anna nodded. When had he noticed that? To her knowledge they hadn't had coffee together more than once since she'd been there. And even then there'd been people milling around. "How do you take yours?"

"However it comes. This is fine." Duncan poured a splash of creamer into his mug and then another into hers.

She reached over and grabbed his hand to tip more into her mug. "There's really no such thing as too much with this."

He chuckled. "Noted."

Anna gave each mug a quick stir and carried them to the small bar-height table in the corner. "Your sister's coming along today."

"Yeah? I'm surprised she has time. I thought she was starting on the bathroom expansion on the second floor today. Plus, she hates garden centers. Or is she dumping us and taking her truck somewhere else?"

"Truck? Oh. Not Deidre. Claire."

"That makes more sense. Though I'm still not sure about the garden center thing. But at least she'll leave us the vehicle and call a ride. She loves that app where you can find someone to drive you wherever you want and you pay them through your phone like you would a taxi. I suspect if she could've figured out how to use them to move, she would have. She's always hated driving."

"Seriously? I mean, I don't love it, but it gets me from A to B." Anna sipped her coffee. How did you live anywhere other than a big city if you didn't like to drive? "Whatever."

Duncan chuckled. "I always managed to make Deidre be the one to tote her around. And it kept Claire from trying to borrow my car, which is definitely a bonus."

"That's true."

"You don't mind, do you?"

Anna looked up and was captured by his gaze. How had she forgotten the potency of his eyes? "What?"

"Claire coming along. Do you mind?"

Yes. "No. Of course not. But you'll have to fight her for shotgun."

A slow grin spread across his features. "Will I? You can't put in a good word with the driver?"

Her heart gave a lazy flip. Oh boy. She took a long drink of coffee. "I'll see what I can do."

"Who's this Danny guy? You're sure Claire's okay with him?" Anna double-checked her seatbelt and looked over at Duncan.

"He's a friend of Jeremiah. You met him."

"Oh. That Danny? He works in Charlottesville? That's quite a commute." She started the engine. "You set? Wait. How does Claire know Danny? She just got here."

Duncan laughed. "She was down shortly after Deidre bought the place. She met him then. I think the four of them went hiking. Maybe they spent more time together too. From what Deidre says, Claire has a bit of a crush. Not sure if it's mutual."

"Ah." Anna shifted into reverse and backed out the parking spot. "Well then, if you're sure she'll be all right grabbing a ride home with him? Back we go."

"Did you get everything you need?" Duncan leaned his seat back a notch and let his head drop to the headrest.

"Yeah, I think so. Had to make a few substitutions, and even then I won't get everything with the big delivery at the end of the week. Where'd you disappear to?"

"After talking with their fountain guy, he convinced me I needed a hardware store more than a garden center. So we went down the road a bit."

"You just got in a car with a stranger?" Anna shook her head. That was something only a man could do. And even then, it didn't seem particularly safe.

He laughed. "He's not exactly a stranger. Marshall Brothers takes jobs all over the state—and in to Maryland and Delaware, to be honest. I've done several commercial properties in Charlottesville, so I've worked with him before. You get to know the people at a garden center like that one. They're really invested in making sure you succeed. And give them referrals."

"Interesting." In her mind, Marshall Brothers was purely a metro D.C. firm. The prospect of jobs outside of that area had never occurred to her. Which, on reflection, was silly. A company with the reputation they had was going to be in high demand, and they'd be fools to turn down jobs that were within an easy commute. Or a short trip, even if the commute wasn't easy. What else had she missed out on by getting caught up in the archives? "So, did *you* get what you need?"

"I hope so. They're going to send it down tomorrow and I guess we'll find out. Tom, that's the water feature guy, had heard of the lion head fountain at Peacock Hill. He was going to go home and do some digging. He thought he had a contact for someone who worked on it ten or fifteen years back. If the guy's still around, it'd be great to pick his brain."

Anna's stomach rumbled. It was just after one and she hadn't had anything but coffee this morning. She'd thought about lunch but hadn't been able to find Duncan. Since she hadn't wanted to drive off and possibly have him thinking she'd left him, she'd made do with a snack-sized candy bar she'd found at the bottom of her purse. "Did you eat lunch?"

"No. Want to drive through somewhere?"

She pulled her lower lip between her teeth. "We could do that. Or...I have a maybe nutty idea."

"Yeah? That sounds promising."

"You say that, but everyone I've ever tried to talk into this has laughed at me."

His eyebrows shot up. "Don't keep me in suspense. I've gotta know, now."

"Do you want to go to Michie Tavern?"

Duncan looked confused. "I'm not sure what that is."

"It was a tavern and hotel of sorts when Thomas Jefferson still lived at Monticello. Now you can tour it and they serve a buffet of eighteenth century recipes. It's over close to Jefferson's house. It's supposed to be delicious." Her face was hot. Was he going to laugh?

"Sure. That sounds fun."

"Really?" Anna grinned, checked her mirrors, and changed lanes. "It's going to take longer than a drive through."

"I don't have anything pressing. Deidre's not in a rush. And it sounds tasty." Duncan pointed out the front window. "There's a sign for Monticello."

She nodded and slid the car into the turn lane at the stop light. "Thanks. Everyone I've tried to get to go says it sounds like something only tourists would do."

Duncan shrugged. "What's wrong with being a tourist? We live in a state that has so much history, seems a shame not to see what you can when you have the chance. And I like food."

Anna laughed. Hopefully the food was good. The website made it look amazing. And they had costumed servers. It sounded fun. Before Duncan asked to tag along, she'd planned to swing by. It'd probably be more fun when someone went with her. Especially when that someone was Duncan.

She wound through Charlottesville and onto the two-lane road that curved up toward Monticello. The tavern appeared on her right as they rounded a bend and she swung into the steeply slanted parking lot. "Nothing quite like parking on a hill."

"It's a slope, that's for sure. Oh, there's a spot."

The parking lot was fullish. A handful of people milled about on the sidewalk. Two tour busses were parked along the hill closest to the road. Anna pulled into the parking space and turned off the car. "Thanks, Duncan."

"I'm always up for an adventure."

That made it...less special, didn't it? Maybe not. He was still here with her. He hadn't laughed at the idea and told her she was ridiculous. Her stomach growled, louder this time. "Which way do you think it is?"

Duncan pointed. "That seems to be where the biggest group of people is."

Anna nodded and started up the hill. They turned where the sidewalk ended next to a man wearing knee pants, long white stockings, a red vest over a cream shirt, and a tri-cornered hat.

"Good afternoon. Are you joining us for lunch?"

"Yes, thank you." Duncan nudged Anna with his elbow.

"Very good, Sir. Just up the steps and through the door."

Anna waited until they'd climbed the first few risers before grinning at Duncan. "This is great. He looked like a coachman, ready to see to our horses."

Laughing, Duncan pulled open the tavern door and gestured for her to go through.

It was like stepping back in time. The walls were rough-hewn wood and the planks of the floor had to be original to the building. A woman in a mob cap and floor-length calico dress greeted them, explained how the meal worked, and pointed them toward the entrance to the serving line. At least it didn't smell old. Instead, it was the scent of fried chicken that was the most pervasive.

"Here's a tray." Duncan set the tray on the rails in front of her and took another for himself. "Smells good, doesn't it?"

"It really does." Anna scooted down the line behind the family in front of them. She spooned a little bit of everything onto her plate as she passed. Fried chicken, as advertised by the aroma, green beans with ham, stewed tomatoes, mashed potatoes and gravy, spoon bread, and a cornbread muffin. She wouldn't need to eat again today, that was certain. A glance over her shoulder showed Duncan's plate was piled even higher than her own.

"Where should we sit?" Duncan peered through the doorway into the front room where they'd entered. "There's a small table here by the fireplace. Want to grab it?"

"Sure." It wasn't cold and, thankfully, the fire wasn't lit. But when she got close, Anna could smell that it was a working fixture in the winter. Tucked in the corner, their table was cozy. Almost romantic. Did this count as a second date? Even if she'd been the one to ask?

The costumed woman who'd greeted them stopped by their table to make sure they knew to let her know if they needed drink refills or seconds of anything.

Duncan took her hand. "Let's pray."

Anna pushed her mind away from the sensation of his hand holding hers and the butterflies that had suddenly taken up residence in her belly and focused on his short blessing. "Amen."

He grinned and picked up the piece of chicken on his plate, biting into it with an audible crunch. Her mouth watered.

"How is it?"

"Really good."

Anna considered her fork and knife briefly. Except...he'd picked his up. And wasn't there some rule about meat on a bone? Besides, he'd seen her covered in dirt—recently and in college—a little chicken grease wasn't going to scare him off. She bit into the succulent bird and sighed. Tourist activity or not, this was worth doing. "I'm so glad you were up for this."

Duncan's eyes lit up. "Me too."

"So. Since my purchases aren't showing up until the end of the week, do you want some help with the fountains?" Anna speared a bite of the green beans and chewed, wrinkling her nose. They tasted fine but they were soggy. She liked hers to have a little crunch to them. And maybe a lot less bacon flavor.

"Sure. Or you could look at the arbor and see about fixing it up." Duncan pushed his beans to the side of his plate. "Whichever. And I was thinking it might be fun to put in a kitchen garden somewhere. There's another building just beyond the arbor—have you walked back that way at all? Deidre says she thinks it was a groundskeeper's cottage, and she's planning to use it for that again once she's up and running. And there's an observation tower, too. Maybe for hunting? But it's livable. We could probably put a kitchen garden near either of those."

"That's kind of far from the actual kitchen though, isn't it?" Anna dipped the tines of her fork into the spoonbread and tasted it. The consistency was almost like pudding. Made of cornbread. Mmm. That was yummy. She scooped a bigger bite.

He shrugged. "I guess. But there's not anyplace closer. Do you think it matters?"

"Only if it's going to be used. No one wants to walk all that way and back to get a sprig of dill. The food would be burned or cold by the time they got back." She frowned. There had to be a better place to put it. "What if we put it in the sunken garden on the right side of the house? That's close to the kitchen back door and it would smell nice. Some of the herbs and such are even pretty."

"That's an idea. We can run it by Deidre and see what she says." He scraped up the last bite of stewed tomatoes and leaned back. "That was delicious."

Anna considered the last bits of food on her plate and pushed it forward a little. "I have another random idea."

"Yeah? This was a good one, let's hear it."

"Want to go see Monticello while we're here?" She held her breath. Was that too much?

He grinned. "Sure. I'm not positive we'll have time to see it all, but why not?"

Anna laughed. It was less about seeing the house where Thomas Jefferson lived than spending more time with Duncan when they weren't supposed to be doing anything specific. He was fun to be around. And when he relaxed, easy to talk to. Another day she'd worry about the fact that she was close to falling in love with him.

8

Duncan mopped the sweat off his forehead and set his tools aside. The right side sunken garden fountain was nearly ready to be tested. For all he'd hoped it would go faster, it had still taken most of the week. But the sound of a delivery truck was unmistakable. He ought to go out front and see if Anna needed help with her delivery.

Anna.

He smiled. Things seemed to be looking up when it came to her. He'd been going out of his way to see her at lunch and dinner. Deidre was never around, though Claire had joined them a couple of times. Even still, they had plenty of time with just the two of them, and he'd enjoyed getting to know her again. Getting to know the woman she'd become. He liked her even more now than he had in college.

"Hey." Duncan stopped beside Anna and peered down the long driveway. A flatbed truck was working its way up the poorly graveled surface.

She flashed a grin. "Hey yourself. Looks like my delivery's on its way. Though I don't see the dump truck with all my soil. Hopefully it's not too far behind, as I need it first."

"We can ask when they get here. If they ever get here."

"They're sure taking their sweet time, aren't they?" Anna chuckled. "Though I guess it's better than leaving a trail of plants behind them on the hill."

The truck rumbled to a stop and the driver pushed open the door and stepped down. "Looking for a Ms. Hamilton?"

"That's me."

The driver produced a clipboard and offered it. "Can you sign here? Where do you want all these?"

"If you go straight past the house, there's a little bit more hill, but that'd be most convenient."

The man frowned. "Can you show me?"

"Sure." Anna handed him the clipboard. "It's just up this way."

The driver strode off behind Anna. Duncan watched them go and walked over to look at the loaded-down truck. She'd gone with more mature plants—that was a good choice. Maybe not so cost effective, but Deidre had given them a generous budget. Was this enough? Pavers were stacked on pallets at one end of the truck. Were those for the paths? Hadn't she been planning on gravel?

"...we'll try to make it, but I can't guarantee with those ruts."

"Okay. Do your best. The less hauling we have to do, the better." Anna came back to stand by Duncan. "Does your sister plan to fix the driveway?"

"It's on her list, but she hasn't made it a priority. Do we need to get her to?"

Anna shrugged. "It's hard to say. Trucks are likely to tear it up some, unless she's paving it. But with how rutted it gets once you're past the house, the driver wasn't sure he could make it very far."

A loud clunking sound came from around the house. Duncan looked at Anna and winced before sprinting off to see the problem. Anna's footsteps pounded behind him.

The truck was stopped half-way up the hill to the upper gardens. The driver crouched by the rear tire.

"Everything okay?" Duncan came to a stop at the truck and peered underneath. Nothing looked damaged from what he could see.

"Think so. But this is where I stop. Sorry, ma'am."

"That's okay. If you can unload everything off to the side, just in case the dirt truck's able to get all the way up, I'd appreciate it." Anna crossed her arms and frowned up the hill.

"I can help you haul everything up when he's gone." Duncan looked at the truck and gave a mental sigh. He'd be sore tomorrow. So would she. That was a lot of material.

"You don't have to do that. I'll just grab it as I need it. And if the soil doesn't show up, I won't need any of it today anyway." Anna puffed out her cheeks and let the air escape noisily. "I'm ready to start making progress."

He smiled. That was a feeling he understood very well. "Anything I can do to help?"

"Nah. I've got it. You might as well get back to work. You've actually got something worth doing. I can babysit this."

"Sure?"

"Yeah, go. When it's all unloaded, I'll come find you. Maybe we can talk more about the kitchen garden."

Duncan nodded and strode away. He wanted to stay and help, but he didn't want to be pushy. Or to come across as being the pushy guy she'd considered him in college. Because he wanted things to work with her. More than he'd anticipated.

"Where've you been?" Deidre stood in the sunken garden, peering at the exposed pipes.

"Anna's truck came, I went to see if I could help. It can't get up the back hill because of the ruts, so we'll have to cart the stuff up manually."

Deidre winced. "Sorry. I'll bump the driveway up on my list. I'm just not sure what I want to do yet."

"Whatcha' need?"

She shrugged and tucked her hands in her pockets, then she started pacing. "I don't know. I'm just struggling, I guess. What am I doing?"

"What do you mean?"

"With this." She gestured expansively at the house. "Am I really going to be able to make something of this? The renovations, sure, I can do those. But then what? What makes me think I can turn this into a retreat center and wedding venue?"

Duncan crossed the garden and sat on one of the steps, patting the space next to him. "You took Dad's little handyman service and turned it into a multi-team company that attracted the notice of a major TV production company."

"And then had to close it because of the contract I signed." Deidre dropped onto the step and propped her elbows on her knees. "Whoopie."

He chuckled. "Okay, so it didn't end the way you might have liked. But for several years you had a thriving, successful business. I think you can do it again. So does Claire. If we didn't, we wouldn't be down here helping."

"But you're not staying. You have Marshall Brothers waiting for you when you get back to D.C."

That was true. Mostly. His job was still there. But did he want it? That was the big question. And he didn't have an answer for it yet. He was praying God would make it clear while he was at Peacock Hill. "You've been praying about it?"

Deidre sighed. "Yeah."

"So you keep doing that. And you remember that I'm here, and Claire is here, because we believe in you. And...I'm not convinced I'll be going back to Marshall Brothers. You know I was unhappy there lately. Maybe it's time for a change." Was there a change that might include Anna in it? He'd keep praying about that, too.

"Seeing you and Jeremiah together, I have to believe you're here because it's where God wants you."

"He's pretty great, isn't he?"

"He's certainly the first boyfriend you've had who I haven't wanted to take out back and punch. So that's a bonus."

She laughed. "Did you really dislike Paul that much? Why didn't I know that?"

"Dad made me promise to keep quiet. Neither of us cared for him, to be honest, but you seemed so happy. And then afterward, there wasn't any point in making you sadder." Duncan bumped his sister's shoulder with his own. "But Jeremiah's great. I look forward to being able to call him my brother some day."

Pink flared on her cheeks. "Do you think so?"

"I really do. Which means you'll get at least one chance to plan and host a wedding here before trying to make a business of it. Chin up, sis. If you're focusing on your relationship with Jesus, He's going to steer you the way He wants you to go."

"I knew you'd know what to say. Thanks, Duncan." Deidre stood and dusted off the back of her jeans. "The fountain on the other side looks nice—it has a soothing sound. Will this one be the same?"

"Should be. If I ever get it working again."

"And that's my cue." She grinned. "See you at dinner?"

"I do like to eat."

"Ask Anna if she'll come. We'll have a housemate-planning meeting."

"Okay." He watched his sister disappear around the front of the house and went back to the exposed pipes that led from the house to the fountain. Checking for leaks was a slow, tedious process. Maybe he should just replace the whole system. Except...generally the pipes were in good shape, and there was always the chance he'd break something that was working if he did a wholesale replacement.

He sat back on his heels. Focus on his relationship with Jesus. That was good advice for both of them.

The scent of Claire's marinara sauce permeated the main floor when Duncan finally dragged himself inside. The fountain was mostly working. The water wasn't flowing as freely as he'd expected, based on the first one he fixed. It could be just the design of this spouting fish, which was different. Or there was something partially clogged inside the statuary. He'd have to send a plumbing snake through it and see if that did anything. But that was tomorrow's job. Now he wanted a long, hot shower and an evening with a book. As he climbed the first step of the grand staircase, his sisters' laughter spilled out of the kitchen.

"There you are. Dinner's ready in about ten."

His shoulders fell. Duncan nodded at Claire and continued up toward the third floor. Hopefully the shower could at least still be hot, since he was losing out on the rest of his evening plans. As he passed the second floor, he heard the water running in the hall bathroom and sighed. The water heater wasn't huge. If Deidre was already downstairs and Anna was showering now...he dragged his mind away from where that thought wanted to take him with a quick prayer. Maybe it was a good thing the water was likely to be cooler than he preferred.

He finished climbing the stairs and headed down the hall to the only semi-finished room on this floor of the house. At least the bathroom was connected. Although, with the girls all sharing, it made sense to have theirs in the hall. Deidre planned to make *en suite* bathrooms where she could, but some of the guests were going to have to share. It simply wasn't feasible to have that much plumbing added—not when she wanted to retain the charm and feel of the original structure. Tearing out all the walls and adding new rooms...that wasn't the way to preserve. Was that one of the reasons she'd steered away from a bed and breakfast?

Duncan shrugged and kicked his bedroom door shut. None of that changed the work he was doing outside. She'd need gardens no matter what she did with the house. He crossed to the bathroom and spun the handle of the shower all the way to hot. The pipes rattled for a second before water shot out. He smiled. Something she'd done had at least upped the output from the anemic trickle he'd been dealing with.

It didn't take long for Duncan to shower and change. The water wasn't icy, but it was only a few shaky steps away from that temperature. It didn't encourage lingering, that was certain. He eyed the growing pile of dirty laundry in the corner. He was going to need to deal with that this weekend, too. There were two washers and dryers set up in the basement, thanks to the previous owners. Deidre insisted they worked fine, but he'd taken his clothes into Waynesboro to the Laundromat the first time he'd needed to wash them. Maybe it was time to give the basement setup a try. He'd start a load tomorrow before heading out to the garden. He ran his comb through his hair and tossed it by the sink. Should he shave? He had a couple days' worth of stubble. He reached for his razor, and then pulled back. It was just a spaghetti dinner. With his sisters. Besides, Anna had seen him working. There was no need to primp.

Muscles protesting, he jogged back down the stairs to the kitchen. Anna, Deidre, and Claire were already at the table with steaming plates of noodles drowning in thick, red sauce in front of them.

"Sorry. I'm late." Duncan angled to the stove and picked up the empty plate that was sitting out. "You can go ahead and start."

"We can wait. I only just sat down." Anna smiled.

Duncan scooped noodles onto his plate before ladling sauce over them and heading to the table. At least the seat next to Anna was open. "This smells amazing, Claire."

"How do you know I didn't make it?" Deidre grinned.

Duncan laughed. "Because I've eaten what you call cooking and it smells nothing like this."

Deidre shook her head. "I'm getting a little better. But you're also not wrong."

"Well, I'm happy to give you lessons if that's what you're after. But only if you're actually interested." Claire reached for the bottle of Parmesan cheese in the middle of the table and shook a generous dusting over her food. "Who's saying the blessing?"

"I can." Anna cleared her throat.

Deidre and Claire bowed their heads. Duncan slid his hand over and curled his fingers lightly around Anna's as she began to pray. Her fingers twitched, almost like a little squeeze. Or was it surprise? She didn't pull away, so he was going to stop over-analyzing it.

When the prayer was over, Anna tugged her hand free and reached for her fork.

Across the table, Deidre's eyebrows shot up, but she didn't say anything. Claire had apparently been too busy cutting up her spaghetti to notice. Just as well. He'd rather not have both of his sisters asking questions he didn't know how to answer.

"Thanks for making time for dinner. I had a little breakdown earlier—Duncan can tell you about that if you need the details—and I realized I needed to spend some time with you guys away from the project." Deidre spun her fork in her noodles before lifting a perfectly swirled bite to her lips.

"I get your sister and brother...but me?" Anna frowned. "I can take this and eat in my room, if you were worried about me feeling left out."

"Seriously?" Claire set down her fork and pinned Anna with her gaze. "You've been here almost three weeks. Now, granted, I haven't been here as long, but even before I arrived I was getting texts from my sister about what an asset you were."

Duncan coughed, tiny flecks of noodle escaping from behind his hand as he tried not to choke.

"What?" Claire pushed a glass of water across the table to Duncan.

"Just thinking of Deidre texting someone. On purpose. It made me laugh and then almost choke to death." He picked up the glass and gulped. "Go on. Sorry."

"I'm getting better at it," Deidre mumbled before taking another bite.

Claire huffed and turned back to Anna. "My point was simply that—to family at least—it's obvious Deidre considers you a friend. Which means I do, too. And it's also obvious Duncan's already moved completely past friendship. So the whole eating in your room thing is just rude."

Duncan's face burned. Claire had always seen more than he realized. It'd be good for him to remember that.

"Sorry." Anna dabbed at the corner of her mouth with her napkin. "I'm not used to being part of a group."

Deidre waved that away. "Now that that's cleared up, I just wanted to thank you—each of you—for believing in me. And Peacock Hill. I'm not sure that I'd go beyond getting it fixed up without you."

"Yes, you would. But I'm still glad you're letting me be part of it." Claire grinned before digging into her pasta again.

"I tend to agree with Claire. You've never been one to walk away from something once you get your teeth into it." Duncan shrugged. "And even though I'm not part of your long-term staffing plan, I'm proud of what this place is going to be."

"You could be, you know." Deidre pointed her fork at her brother. "I'm going to need someone around to maintain the grounds. And no, it's not the same as what you're doing now, I know that. But there's nothing that says you couldn't do consulting from here. Having your own firm is something you've talked about since the ink was glistening on your diploma. We're close enough to civilization that you could make it work if you didn't mind a little driving."

The idea dangled in front of him like a golden carrot before it evaporated into mist. Who was he kidding? He didn't have the contacts yet to start off on his own. The contacts he did have were primarily up near D.C. Except...there was Charlottesville and the garden center. They'd probably refer business his way. Richmond wasn't that much farther. And if he switched to a residential focus...maybe. It was at least in the realm of a remote possibility. "I...but you'd need a florist on site.

Weren't you thinking of combining the two needs into one position?"

Deidre shrugged. "Maybe. If I have to look for some random person I don't know to take the job, then yeah, I'm going to make sure they can do everything I need. But if I have the possibility of my brother hanging out here? I'll make contacts with nearby florists and work out packages with them instead."

Anna cleared her throat. "If it ends up that Duncan isn't interested, I would be. If the whole florist situation can be dealt with by contractors. Flower arranging isn't an art where I have any skill."

"Yeah?" Deidre grinned. "Cool. Guess I'll add networking with nearby florists to my ever-growing to-do list."

"Nope. Let me handle that." Claire slid her phone out of her pocket and tapped a note. "I'm here for the business side of things, remember? Making friends with other business owners is right up my alley. In fact, since you're thinking wedding venue, once we have a general idea of when you'll be available to take reservations, I thought I'd make up a brochure and go visit some of the bridal shops in Charlottesville and Richmond. You're also going to need a website."

Deidre groaned and buried her head in her hands.

Claire patted her sister's shoulder. "Hey. It's okay. You can do this. It's why you have people helping you though. No one expects you to do it all on your own."

"What Claire said." Duncan grinned and scraped the last bit of sauce from his plate. "You know Mom and Dad would come down and help out, too, if you asked."

"I know." Deidre sighed and scooped up another bite. "I hate to ask, though. They like it up there. But I might need Mom for a little bit when it comes to decorating."

"I thought you had a friend who's a decorator?" Anna pushed her empty plate a few inches toward the center of the table. "Didn't you say something about that in our early emails?"

Claire growled. "That woman is not a friend."

Deidre held up a hand. "I did say that. At the time, I thought she was. Turns out that's not quite the case."

Anna winced. "Sorry."

"I'll fill you in later, if you want." Duncan touched Anna's hand. How did the smallest contact like that set every nerve ending on edge?

"Anyway." Deidre clapped her hands. "Enough business. I want to hear about the field trip you two took on Monday when you were in Charlottesville. It sounds like it might be something I need to do."

Duncan frowned and glanced at Anna, who was grinning and launching into a retelling of their lunch at Michie Tavern and subsequent trip to Monticello. He hadn't mentioned it to Deidre...when had Anna? He studied his sister. Anna seemed to keep her up to date with her comings and goings. Maybe he needed to pull

Deidre aside and see if she had any insight into Anna's heart.

9

Anna's muscles were screaming. The truck full of soil had finally arrived on Friday. So she'd spent all day shoveling into the beds she'd dug. There'd only been enough in the truck to do one of the side gardens, so she'd arranged for another delivery next week. Hopefully by then she'd be able to move without wanting to cry.

She hobbled downstairs to the kitchen. Even though it was Saturday, she had a full day of work in the garden planned. The plants that had arrived on Thursday really needed to be put in. Maybe the work would stretch everything out again. She hadn't ached like this in...ever.

Where was everyone? Usually on Saturdays someone was milling around, indulging in an extra cup of coffee. Anna checked her phone. It was just after eight. Could she possibly be the first person up? She'd only gotten out of bed because she rolled over and everything protested the movement. A hot shower had helped a little. Moving around seemed to be working as well.

Anna poured a cup of coffee and shuffled to the table, with a brief stop at the fridge to grab a container of yogurt.

"Morning." Barely containing a yawn, Duncan pushed through the kitchen door, aiming straight for the coffee. "You're up early."

She smiled. If Duncan thought it was early, then it probably was. He was usually the first one up and out of the house. And the results were well worth it. She'd been taking her breaks in the sunken garden that he wasn't actively working on. The trickle of water was soothing and her imagination took off, picturing what it would look like once he had the plantings done. "I wanted to get started on the shrubs that outline the picture garden."

"Picture garden?" He nodded, sipping from his mug. "I like that. Descriptive and yet fun. What will you call the other side?"

Heat warmed her cheeks. She'd been planning to take the names to Deidre before mentioning them to anyone else. It was, after all, Deidre's final decision. "Um. The chapel garden."

"Nice. Have you run them by Dee yet?"

Anna shook her head and spooned up yogurt.

"She'll like them, too. I can almost guarantee it. Wanna come up with some names to distinguish the sunken gardens? That's not my strong suit." He stood and crossed to the counter, where he dug in the breadbox, eventually emerging with a bagel. He dropped it in the toaster and pressed the lever. "No one is going to want to visit the fish garden."

She laughed. "Probably not. Have you given any thought to the plantings? That might suggest some names."

"Not really. Although, there's the kitchen garden idea we still haven't finalized. And if we do go that route, it's not a bad name."

She didn't want the kitchen garden there. But she couldn't come up with a compelling reason why not, especially after it had been her idea in the first place. It just rankled to use such a pretty, serene space for something like herbs. Of course, there was the other side where relaxing could happen. But... "Yeah. I guess."

"You don't like the idea."

Anna shrugged. "No. But I can't figure out why. Sorry."

"It's okay. So...no kitchen garden? At all, or just put it somewhere else?" Duncan took the bagel out of the toaster and bounced it on his fingers on the way back to the table.

"No butter? Jelly? Cream cheese?"

One corner of his mouth poked up. "Nope."

"Weird."

He laughed.

"Maybe we should look at the places you were considering for the kitchen garden. Though it's still far to walk." She sighed. What was wrong with the sunken garden? It had seemed like a good idea when she first mentioned it. "Or...maybe we could put it at the near edge of the picture garden? Even on the outside of the surrounding hedges?"

"That's an idea. We'll take a look. It's not like we need one. I just thought it might be fun." He crunched into the bagel and chewed. "For all we know, Deidre will nix the idea."

Anna nodded and drained her mug. She slid from the stool-height chair and bit back a groan. The digging today had better work out the kinks or she was going to be immobile tomorrow. "I'm going to get started."

His face fell. "Already?"

"I'm so sore, if I don't start now, I might never get up the energy to do it." Hesitating a moment, she reached out and covered his hand. "Come find me when you're ready and we'll look at spots for the herbs."

Duncan flipped his hand over, caught her fingers, and pulled her closer. Heat from his body sent shivers running through her. Her heart beat like it was trying to explode out of her chest. "Can I take you out tonight? Just you and me?"

Anna stared into his eyes, her nerve endings on fire. She couldn't get her breath to form words so she nodded.

A slow grin spread across his face, and he reached up to touch her cheek. "That might just get me through the day."

Mouth dry, she swallowed.

He released her hand and gave her a little nudge toward the door. "Go get your work done so you're not distracted tonight."

Her legs were jelly. Would they even carry her anymore? Anna made it out of the kitchen then leaned against the wall and closed her eyes. If he could reduce her to mush with a look, what on earth was going to happen if he kissed her?

She couldn't wait to find out.

"Want to go for a walk?"

Anna looked at Duncan's outstretched hand and smiled. She slipped her hand in his. "I really would."

Peacock Hill looked different in the moonlight. It rose, stately and white, from the driveway. Lights burned on the main floor and in the bedroom Claire had claimed on the second. Deidre and Jeremiah had invited them to stay for pizza again with the gang, and they'd exchanged knowing looks when Duncan had demurred. Anna had expected to join them for games when they got back from dinner, if there was still time. A walk, alone in the moonlight, was better. Much better.

"Let's go around this way." He gave her hand a little tug, and they walked around to the left, down the stairs into the sunken garden where the fish fountain was bubbling away.

"That's such a nice sound. I'm glad you could get it working again."

He smiled. "Me, too. I want to show Deidre the plan I worked up for the plantings soon. Maybe Monday. I'd love your opinion. But let's keep walking. I found something the other day, and I wondered if you'd seen it."

"Yeah? What is it?"

He chuckled. "You have to see. Come on."

"Not even a hint?" She laughed as they strolled across the driveway and up the stairs to the elevated lawn where the two side gardens would be located. The hedges she'd planted this morning were dark lumps across the way, and the arbor stretched out in front of them, the chipped white wood glowing in the moonlight.

"Nope." He paused. "This is pretty at night, isn't it?"

"It is. Another few weeks and it won't be dark until close to nine. She could have summer weddings in the evening without any outside lighting. At least out here on the lawn. Once the hedges grow in, it'll probably be too dark in the chapel garden."

"Make sure you mention that to her. It's a good idea." He started walking again. Before long, they'd climbed the two steps to the arbor and stepped down on the other side. "Have you been back here?"

Anna shook her head. "I keep meaning to explore. Then I get caught up."

"Yeah? With what?"

His teasing tone made her grin. Was he fishing? She chuckled. "Oh, this and that. There's this guy I've been seeing."

"Oh? What's he like?"

"Hm. We went to college together. I had a pretty serious crush on him back then, too. But it seems like he's finally noticed me. It's nice."

"I'm willing to bet he noticed you in college."

"He says he did. But he never did anything about it."

"Maybe he regrets that and is trying to do something about that now."

Her heart raced and she stopped, turning to look at him. "I hope so."

Duncan's lips curved. "Just a little farther."

Anna followed him past a little grove of pine trees and drew in a breath. "Oh, wow."

"Right?"

She couldn't call it a pond. It was probably too small to be anything official. But it was surrounded by dogwood trees, most of which still carried some blooms on their branches. "I wish I'd seen this two weeks ago. Those blooms must've been spectacular."

"I was thinking we should talk Deidre into putting some benches between the trees. It'd make a perfect spot to get away from everything at the house and read or think. Or..." He turned to face her and brushed a strand of hair off her cheek. His gaze locked with hers as he eased closer.

Her heart thundered in her chest. As his lips touched hers, her eyes fluttered closed. She leaned closer and wound her arms around his waist, the contact sending heat and sparks through her.

"Yep. Definitely a good place to do that." Duncan didn't step back or loosen his embrace.

"I don't know."

He frowned.

Anna fought a grin. "Maybe we ought to do it again, just to be sure."

"That's an experiment I can get behind." Laughing, Duncan lowered his lips to hers.

It really was too bad she couldn't carry a tune, because her heart was singing. Anna grinned as she stomped her shovel into the soil to deepen the hole she was working on. Duncan McIntyre. It was like a dream. *He* was like a dream. Maybe it was good they'd never gotten together in college. Although...there were a lot of wasted years now.

She tossed the shovel aside and reached for the potted azalea. It wasn't blooming yet, but when it did it would be the perfect pop of color for this section of the picture garden. She lowered the plant into the hole and filled it. This was the last photo area she had planned. Once it was planted, all that would be left was to gravel the paths.

The truckload of white pebbles had arrived yesterday, so it was down to hauling wheelbarrows full of the stuff and raking it into place, and then setting the pavers as stepping stones. That would take at least a day. The chapel garden would see her through the end of the week. And then...Anna sighed. Then she probably had to head back to Richmond and her job at the archives. She could possibly stretch it a few days into next week. But her boss had been clear that she needed to be back at her desk on June first.

She grabbed the shovel and started on another hole. The work would be done. But...Duncan. What was she supposed to do about him? Would he stay here or head back to D.C.?

"This is looking great." Deidre grinned. "I really like the windy paths you put in. Is that big pile of rock for the paths?"

Anna nodded.

"Nice. Classy." She paused and licked her lips. "So, I realize it's probably none of my business."

Uh oh. Nothing good ever started that way. Anna clenched the handle of the shovel.

"I was wondering about you and my brother."

"What about us?"

"Well. You said you had to be back at work in June, right? That's coming up. I just...had you thought about it at all?" Deidre shoved her hands in her pockets. "I'm probably making a mess of this."

"No. Not really. Thought about it? Yes. It's pretty much all I can think about. But I'm not sure what to do. I have to have a job, and it's in Richmond. Along with my apartment and all that. Besides, isn't he heading back to D.C.?"

Deidre shrugged. "I don't get the feeling he wants to. He's muttering to himself as he's digging in plants in the sunken gardens. That's never a good sign."

"What do you mean?"

"That's how he works through sticky problems."

Like her? Was she a problem he had to work through? If she was, was that a good thing? "Oh."

Deidre laughed. "You two really are a pair. Getting information out of you is like digging into the secrets of the Illuminati."

"The Illuminati?" Anna snorted. "What are you reading these days?"

Deidre blushed. "So I like thrillers. Sue me. Even Jeremiah makes fun of me. Then he asks to borrow them."

"Aww. You two are so cute."

"Thanks." Deidre frowned. "And nice job with the distraction technique. It almost worked. You're not going to break up with my brother when you go back to Richmond, are you? Please say no. You're the first girl he's dated who I like. And I hate to make him feel awkward by being your friend when you're not together."

Anna blinked as she worked her way through that convoluted mess. "No. I don't plan to break up with him. Ever. And I like you, too."

"Yay!" Deidre clapped. "Claire likes you too, by the way. Obvs."

"Obvs? What is that?"

"Obviously? Jeremiah's trying to teach me to text."

Anna laughed. "Maybe save the abbreviations for actual texting."

"Got it. Oh. Hey. Girls' night Friday?"

Her last Friday here? "I was thinking Duncan and I..."

"Oh, no. Jeremiah's having a guys' night and is going to rope Duncan into it. So you're not missing out on a chance to hang with him at Make-Out Lake."

Anna's jaw dropped. "Where?"

"That little pond behind the arbor. Duncan took me out there and mentioned that he showed it to you Saturday night. There's no way there wasn't kissing going on."

"I'm not even going to dignify that with a response." Anna stuck the shovel back into the ground. "I should get back to work."

"Mmmhmm. Make-Out Lake. I should take Jeremiah back there some evening." Deidre winked. "Friday at five. Don't forget."

"Maybe." She was going to talk to Duncan first. If he wiggled out of guys' night, she wouldn't mind missing out on girl time. She focused on digging the hole for the next azalea. When she looked up, Deidre had left. Anna situated the bush and filled in around its roots, then tossed the shovel aside. She'd go find Duncan now and ask about Friday. Her lips twitched.

And maybe try to talk him into a little field trip to the pond.

10

Duncan parked at the curb in front of a little bungalow that looked like it had been sitting right where it was for at least sixty years. It wasn't shabby. In fact, it was meticulously neat. But the style spoke clearly of days gone by, when plaid bell-bottoms were all the rage and people actually considered mustard yellow a reasonable color. The landscaping wasn't bad. Predictable, perhaps, but functional. He got out of the car and followed the path to the front door, imagining a few tweaks that would give the space a unique look and add to the curb appeal.

Jeremiah threw open the front door before Duncan got to it. "I was beginning to wonder if you were going to bail on us."

"Am I late?" Duncan reached for his phone to check the time.

"No, you're right on time. But your sister has mentioned your habit of being ten minutes early everywhere you go." Jeremiah clapped Duncan on the shoulder. "Come on in. I've got root beer and other assorted sodas in the fridge. Make yourself at home."

At home. Where he'd rather be. He could be walking the property with Anna, as they'd taken to doing in the evenings. They'd found hiking trails and clearings and were working on convincing Deidre to get them officially mapped so her guests could wander. There was a large clearing that would be perfect for evening bonfires just past the stone tower that rose three stories at the back of what he considered the yard. Deidre—or another staff person—would need to be in charge of those, but she could set up tables with s'more fixings. Retreat groups would love that sort of thing.

Duncan followed Jeremiah through the entry hall and into the den. Wide-planked, distressed wood floors flowed through the entire space. Not a strand of shag carpeting to be found. "This is nice. Lot of work?"

"Oh yeah. But it's mostly elbow grease, not a lot of know-how. Except those." Jeremiah jerked his chin in the direction of the kitchen.

Duncan wandered over and ran a hand over the counters. At first glance, they'd looked like granite. But they didn't feel like it. And when you looked closer... "Concrete? Nice. My sister did a big online tutorial for concrete countertops once."

"Pretty sure that's the one I used. I know about the whole *Flippin' for You* deal."

"Of course." Paul Rossi, the host of the show who was also Deidre's former boyfriend, had made a nuisance of himself when Deidre first bought Peacock Hill. Duncan had been tempted to drive down then and explain, in short words punctuated with a few well-placed shoves, exactly where Paul needed to take himself. But his sister had handled it. She could handle anything. "They turned out well."

"That's what she said. I think they might be what finally got her to seriously consider dating me." Jeremiah grinned. "So I'm partial to them. I'll be sad to let them go when I move out."

"Move?" Duncan frowned. Was everyone deserting his sister down here? Maybe he needed to reconsider going back to D.C.

Red colored Jeremiah's cheeks. "Eventually. After—look, you know I'm serious about your sister, right?"

Duncan nodded. That was why the moving comment was so concerning.

"Be right back." Jeremiah hurried down the hallway on the far side of the den.

Since there was a big tub of ice with bottles and cans in it on the counter, Duncan poked around. Root beer in a bottle. He hadn't had that in a while. He pulled one out and dried it on the edge of his shirt before twisting off the cap and taking a sip.

"I have this." Jeremiah thrust a small, velvet box at him.

Duncan set down his bottle and took it. "Is this...?"

Jeremiah nodded. "Open it."

Duncan flipped open the lid. His eyes widened at the sight of the enormous solitaire set flush in a thick gold band. "She could wear this and still work."

"That was the idea. There's very little to catch on things. Of course, if she's using a saw or laying tile, she should take it off. I got a chain to go with it. It's in the bottom of the box." Jeremiah clasped his hands. "Do you think she'll like it?"

"She'd be an idiot not to. And my sister's no idiot." Duncan handed back the box.

"Hello?" The door slammed and Matt stomped into the den. His gaze traveled back and forth between Duncan and Jeremiah. "Am I interrupting something?"

"Ha. Ha." Jeremiah offered the box to Matt. "I mentioned this to you the other day."

Matt took the box and shook his head. "You've got it bad."

"Got what bad?" Sock-footed, Danny padded into the room. "Oh, wow. Let me see that."

Matt handed Danny the box and headed for the tub of drinks. "Now that we've established that there's entirely too much love in the air around here, can we move on to more manly pursuits?"

Danny punched Jeremiah in the shoulder and handed back the ring. "When are you giving it to her?"

"I don't know yet. It still seems too soon." Jeremiah tucked the ring in his pocket. "Maybe in the fall?"

Too soon to give his sister the ring, but not too soon to buy it? His dad, at least, would be glad if they waited 'til fall—or longer—to get engaged. Knowing Deidre, she'd want to get married as quickly as she could arrange it. Duncan gave a mental shrug and pushed it out of his mind. He didn't care beyond knowing Jeremiah was a good guy and seemed ideally suited for his sister. Beyond that, they just needed to tell him what to wear and when to show up. "What manly pursuits were you talking about, Matt?"

Matt gave an exaggerated sigh. "Newbies. We keep inviting newbies."

"Hey! If we're evaluating the newbie status of the people in the room other than Duncan, that leaves you." Danny drilled a finger into Matt's chest as he walked into the kitchen for a root beer.

"Not anymore. Now we have Duncan." Matt grinned. "Where are the snacks? I can smell nachos, but I don't see them."

Jeremiah chuckled and pointed to the oven. "I left them in there so they'd stay warm. And as for manly pursuits, with Matt that generally means a video game wherein you play football with more skill than you ever maintained in gym class."

"Whatever. I seem to recall one of us actually made the team. And, oh yeah, it wasn't you." Matt crossed to the oven and opened it. He looked around and, after a second, grabbed a towel off the counter which he used as a pot holder to bring a gigantic tray of nachos out of the oven. "This is what I'm talking about."

"Jeremiah's a bit of a nacho superstar around here. You'll understand when you get some." Danny nudged Duncan in the ribs. "Better get a plate fast, though, or Matt'll eat 'em all."

"One time. There was one time I ate the last serving of nachos without asking. Am I ever going to live it down?"

"Pfft. Please. You know the answer to that." Jeremiah took a stack of plates out of a cupboard and set them on the counter by the food before opening the fridge and retrieving several containers. "Toppings galore—help yourself."

Nachos weren't really his thing, but Duncan took a plate off the stack and waited for Matt to load his and move out of the way. They did smell good—probably the cows-worth of cheese melted all over them—so that was something. He managed to only burn two fingers sliding a generous portion onto his plate before eyeing the toppings. Jeremiah had a serious salsa problem. "Why do you have four kinds of salsa? It's salsa."

"Dude." Jeremiah shook his head and pointed to the jars. "There's something for everyone here, if you mix properly. Are you a spicy guy? Mild? More in it for the flavor?"

"Uh. I haven't put that much thought into it. I don't generally like nachos."

Danny and Matt both stopped and stared, jaws agape.

Jeremiah frowned. "You haven't had the right nachos, then."

"That's what Deidre's always saying." Duncan shrugged. "It's chips with stuff on it. It's not like it's—"

"I'm going to stop you before you embarrass yourself." Jeremiah scooped from three bottles of salsa and spread the contents across Duncan's plate. He proceeded to the sour cream, guacamole, and other toppings. "Here. Now you have real nachos."

Duncan looked at the pile of food. "Do you have a fork?"

"Sure. In the drawer by the sink. You're still going to get messy, you know that, right?"

"Probably." Duncan sighed and grabbed a fork before taking a seat at the kitchen table by Matt, who was shoveling nachos into his mouth with his fingers. It was going to be a long night.

"Have fun last night?" Deidre detoured to ruffle his hair on her way to the coffee pot.

"Yeah."

"You sound surprised."

"I guess I am, a little. I'm a lot older than those three. I didn't honestly believe we'd have anything in common." Duncan shrugged. "But it was good. Even though they have some weird fixation with nachos."

Deidre laughed. "I should've warned you. Or them."

"Probably them. Although I will admit that Jeremiah's nachos are the best I've ever had. But I'm still not signing up to eat them on any kind of regular basis."

He scraped the last bite of eggs off his plate. "How about you? Fun night?"

"Definitely." Deidre carried her mug over to the table and sat, stealing a triangle of toast off his plate. "I like Anna a lot. And she's so in love with you. It's fun to see."

Was she? The thought made him warm all the way through. He hadn't allowed himself to use the L-word. Not even in his mind. But it was always there, lurking. "I could say the same about Jeremiah."

She sighed, a dreamy smile on her face. "He's so great."

Duncan snorted. "I can practically see little stars in your eyes."

"Your jealousy does no good." She bit into the toast and made a face. "Cinnamon and sugar? Are you twelve?"

"No one offered it to you." He smiled and bit into the other piece. "Mmmmm."

"Blech." Deidre put the piece she'd stolen back on his plate. "What are you up to today?"

"Maybe the arbor. It looks like it just needs to be scraped and repainted. None of the columns are rotted, which is a minor miracle. The wisteria should be here Monday. And...that's the last landscaping project. I figured I'd head back to D.C. on Wednesday."

Deidre's face fell. "You're not going to stay?"

He ran a hand over his face. "I have to go back and tie up all the loose ends at a minimum. But...I don't know what to do."

"What does Anna say?"

"She doesn't say anything. I keep waiting for her to say something—anything. And I get crickets. I was hoping...I don't know...for something obvious. But she has a job to get back to, too. Maybe we just have to wait and see what happens."

Deidre frowned. "Long distance relationships never last."

"They can. And she's only what, two hours away? It's not like she's in another state. Or country. I don't know what else to do." Duncan finished his toast and carried his plate to the sink.

"Stay here. Didn't Jeremiah talk to you about helping with the landscaping projects he gets hired for? He said he was going to."

He nodded. And it was a possibility. But a handful of jobs did not a sustainable career make. Especially when he was looking at the prospect of a wife and kids.

Where had that thought come from? Wife, sure. He'd been having that thought about Anna for years. Even when he was convinced she had no interest in him at all. But kids? That was a new wrinkle that added only confusion. "I don't know, Dee."

She sighed. "At least talk to Anna about it before she leaves?"

"Okay. Any idea when that's going to be?"

"She hasn't told you?"

He shook his head.

"Tomorrow afternoon."

His heart sank. He'd known it was coming—even that it was likely to be this weekend. And yet he'd been hoping for some kind of reprieve. A clear sign that would show him how they could be together. A month wasn't long enough for feelings as strong as he had. Except that they'd started ten years ago, and they'd never gone away. She'd claimed his heart in college and reclaimed it at Peacock Hill. "I'll try."

11

Anna trailed her fingers along the newly planted shrubs. When everything had grown in and was in bloom it was going to be amazing. Would she be here to see it? Of course not. But she could visit. The women's group at church was always looking for new places to hold their weekend retreats. Maybe by the time the next one rolled around, Peacock Hill would be open for business.

Her eyes filled. The last month had been the best she'd had since college. And not completely because of Duncan, though he was certainly a factor. Deidre and Claire were, too. And even Mrs. Patterson at church, despite the fact that it felt like she was looking for internal flaws to point out. But beyond all the people, having a chance to finally do what she'd set out to do had reminded her exactly why she'd gotten that degree in the first place. And now...she'd go back to the archives and her online master's in library science program. The one she was a semester away from finishing but she kept finding reasons to put off.

Anna blinked rapidly. A tear escaped and she swiped at it with the back of her hand. She didn't want to be a librarian. Or work at the archives. She could apply to firms again like she had right after college. Except...no one had wanted her then. Now she was ten years out of her degree program with very little relevant work experience. Why would they want her now?

"There you are. I've been looking for you." Duncan slid his arms around her from behind and kissed the top of her head.

She stiffened.

"What's wrong?"

The concern in his voice pushed more tears from her eyes and she shook her head, not trusting her voice.

"Hey." Duncan nudged her shoulder until she turned to face him. "Talk to me."

Anna shook her head. "I just...hate my job. I don't want to go back. But what else is there to do? You're going to be here, and it's not that much of a drive..."

"I won't, though. I have to go back to D.C. But that's not much farther."

She searched his face. "You're not taking the job here? Why wouldn't you?"

"I'm not set against it. But I need to pray about it more. I wanted more clear-cut direction." He pressed his lips together. "You should do it. Talk to Deidre. You know she'd hire you in an instant. And then you'd get to hang around and see all your plant babies grow up and thrive."

"What about you?"

He shrugged. "I'll be okay at Marshall Brothers. I have a client base who loves me and, if I have to, I'll go above my boss' head to keep him from stealing the work for his cronies."

"You'll hate it." The few times he'd talked about his job, he'd mentioned how much he disliked the new boss. And how unhappy he and his past clients were with the job disposition.

"I'll live. There are other firms out there, for that matter. If it gets too bad I can always find somewhere else to work. I should dust off my resume, just in case. And if I do that, I could move to Charlottesville or Richmond. That'd at least be a little closer to you."

His words left her warm and cozy. He wanted to be near her. She rested her head on his shoulder. "Closer is good. You really wouldn't mind if I talked to Deidre?"

"'Course not. You should be working in the field, not answering reference desk questions. You're talented. And there are so many other spots on this property that could use some landscaping. If you can talk Deidre into it." Duncan pulled her close, his arms tightening around her. "I'll miss seeing you every day."

Her heart constricted. "I'll miss you, too. When do you think you can come down to visit?"

"I'm not sure. Not this weekend, most likely. Maybe next."

She nodded. "Maybe in Richmond? I'll need to give notice. And pack. And that's assuming your sister's on board with it. I'm not a florist, remember?"

"Talk to her. She was open to it before. I'm sure she still is." His hands moved up and down her back. Soothing her.

Could they make a long-distance relationship work? Occasional weekends and phone calls would help but...was that enough? "I wish we could both stay down here."

"So do I, Anna. So do I." His lips found hers.

She sighed and sank into the embrace. She'd take the now and worry about the future later. If God wanted them to be together, He'd make a way for it to happen. Wouldn't He?

"I'm sorry to hear you're leaving, dear." Mrs. Patterson took Anna's hand and patted it. "I heard you did some mighty fine work up at Peacock Hill. I imagine you would've liked to see it all grown in."

"Yes, ma'am." More than the woman could possibly know. She hadn't found a chance to talk to Deidre yet. Would she get one before she had to leave? Her boss at the archives had called her twice during church. Probably checking to be sure Anna would be in the office at eight a.m. sharp tomorrow morning. Had anyone been doing archive requests since she left? "I hope to come back and visit. Frequently."

"Do that. And be sure you make it to church when you do." Mrs. Patterson smiled, patted her hand again, and wandered off.

Duncan snuck up behind her and whispered in her ear. "She's something, isn't she?"

"That she is. She's Matt's grandmother?"

"I think that's what Jeremiah said. I don't remember exactly." Duncan turned to look out at the emptying parking lot then back to Anna. "Do you have time for lunch before you go?"

Did she? Her car was packed. She needed to talk to Deidre, but otherwise...it was only a couple of hours to Richmond. "Yeah. I'd like that."

He grinned and took her hand. "Did you talk to my sister at all?"

"Not yet. That's the last thing I need to do before I go." She frowned. "I caught a ride with Deidre and Claire...did they leave already?"

Duncan held up a set of keys. "Deidre went with Jeremiah and asked me to drive her truck back. Claire took my car."

"Why didn't Claire take Dedire's car?"

He laughed. "Deidre doesn't trust her with the truck since she does so little driving."

"Poor Claire."

"Not really. If I had any other option, I wouldn't have given her my keys. She's not a bad driver. But...I like my car."

Anna shook her head. "Where are we eating?"

"It's a surprise."

Her eyebrows lifted. "I need to be on the road by three."

"I can make that happen. Come on." He led her down the steps and across the parking lot to Deidre's truck.

"Does she always have that much stuff in the truck bed? Isn't that dangerous?"

Duncan held the door open for her. "Why would it be dangerous?"

"Doesn't it fly out or something?"

He laughed and shook his head as he closed the door.

Great. Was she supposed to know all about pickups? When he climbed into the driver's seat, she shifted to look at him. "I sound like an idiot, don't I?"

"Nope. Sometimes paper or something will fly out. But, generally, you don't put it back there if it's not heavy enough to stay." He started the engine and backed out of the spot. "Off we go."

"Do I get a hint, at least, of where we're headed?"

He shook his head and steered onto the highway. "You'll see soon enough."

Anna sighed. "It's so pretty out here. Richmond is nice, but it's a city. This though...it's restful. Even on the highway."

"I guess there's a reason Peacock Hill was built out here. Even back then people needed to get away from the city and breathe in the mountain air." Duncan flicked the turn signal and exited where the sign said "Skyline Drive."

How was it that she'd been out here for a month and hadn't made time to go on even one hike? Oh, that's right. Duncan. And the job. But mostly Duncan.

The road wound up the mountain, gradually tapering into a smoother scenic drive.

"It shouldn't be far." Duncan checked to the right as he drove. "Keep an eye out for a turn in, would you?"

Anna looked out her window at the wall of trees. Beautiful. Up ahead she saw a break in the foliage. "I think there's one right here?"

He slowed and flipped on the turn signal. "Yeah. That looks like the right one. You up for a short hike or do you want to just sit at a picnic table?"

Anna looked down at the ballet flats she'd worn to church. "What kind of hike? If it's a short walk on a path, I can do that. If we're talking climbing over rocks and fallen logs, then probably not."

"Hmm. They said it was a trail. That, to me at least, says dirt. Wanna go a little bit and see how you do? We can always turn back and claim a picnic table."

She nodded. "Sure. That sounds like a plan."

He grinned and pushed open his door. "I'll grab the food."

Anna smiled. He'd planned ahead. What would he have done if she'd said no to lunch? He probably had some kind of back-up plan in place. That seemed like something he'd do. She hopped down from the truck and met Duncan at the back.

"Ready?"

She nodded and slipped her hand into his. "This is nice. Thanks."

"My pleasure. I'm sorry I didn't think of it sooner." He squeezed her hand. "I think it's right over this way."

They crossed the parking lot and found the trail head. The packed dirt path was reasonably walkable in her shoes, though she wouldn't want to do it every day. Every rock made its presence known. At least it wasn't painful.

"How are you doing?"

"Good. If it stays like this, I should be fine. Where are we headed?"

"Jeremiah said there's a waterfall not too far down this way. I thought that sounded like a good place to have our last lunch."

Her stomach dropped. That sounded so final. Like an ending. "For a while, at least."

"For a while." He squeezed her hand again.

They walked along in comfortable silence. Occasionally, one of them would point out a bird or squirrel they spotted as they walked. Before long, the quiet burble of water reached their ears and, as they walked around a bend in the trail, they came to it. Water flowed down rocks to a stream that led off into the forest at the base of the hill that had risen ahead of them.

"Oh. Look at that." Anna stopped and took in the view. "This was a good idea."

Duncan set his backpack down and unzipped it. He pulled out a blanket and spread it on the ground. "M'lady."

Anna laughed. Where had that come from? She lowered herself to the blanket and crossed her legs. "Can I help?"

"Nope. I've got this." Duncan sat across from her and continued unloading the backpack. "Okay. We have chicken salad that can either be put on a bed of lettuce or made into a sandwich. There's slices of melon and dessert is a secret."

"Yum. I think I'll go sandwich." Anna reached for the chicken salad and scooped some onto the slices of bread Duncan offered. She took a big bite and smiled. "Did you make this?"

"I have a few skills in the kitchen. Very few, mind you, but chicken salad is one of them. The key is to find a good rotisserie chicken for the base. After that it's easy." Duncan prepped his own sandwich before reaching for her hand. "Can I pray?"

Heat flooded her face. She ought to have waited. "Of course."

"Heavenly Father, thank you for this meal and the beautiful day we have to share it. Be with Anna as she drives to Richmond later this afternoon and have Your hand on our relationship as it moves forward into this new phase. Help us to know Your will for us as a couple and in our individual careers. Amen."

"Amen." Anna sighed and took another bite. Was her inability to talk to Deidre a sign of some sort, or just bad timing? At the rate she was going, it didn't seem likely that she'd manage the conversation before she needed to be on the road. Most Sundays, Deidre was nowhere near Peacock Hill until dinner. And Anna needed to be gone before that. "I'm still not sure what to do."

"About?"

"My job. They rely on me at the archives. I'm the only one who can help with plant identification and the finer points of...and it's just so boring. But they need me. Am I letting them down if I leave?"

Duncan frowned. "I don't know. Are you letting yourself down if you stay?"

Whew. That...was a question. Was she? "I hadn't thought of it that way."

"I'll pray that you have direction. I hope you'll do the same for me?"

"Of course." Words lodged in her throat. Anna didn't want to leave him, and yet their time was coming to a close. Would they survive a long-distance relationship? Her feelings hadn't faded in the years since college. Duncan said his hadn't either. But would they continue to grow if they were apart? Fighting tears, she set her sandwich aside. "Duncan? I'm going to miss you."

12

"You're set?" Deidre leaned on the door frame of Duncan's third-floor bedroom.

He zipped his duffel closed and nodded. "Last thing to go right here. And your landscaping is in good shape now. Everything needs to grow in a little, but you could have a wedding tomorrow and it'd look good."

Her smile didn't reach her eyes. "I know. Thanks. I just wish you were staying."

"I do, too. And who knows...maybe I'll end up back this way anyway. I had another email from my boss this morning. Things don't look good." Duncan sighed. He needed clear direction. So did Anna. But what happened if both of them ended up thinking the job at Peacock Hill was the answer to their problems? "Did you talk to Anna before she left?"

"No. She was gone by the time I got back from Jeremiah's parents' house. Why?"

"She was going to talk to you about coming back and handling the garden work."

Deidre drew her brows together. "I wonder why she didn't leave a note. Or call. Except...I'd rather hold out for you."

"And I appreciate that. But she might be free sooner than I am. And she's just as good. You've seen that for yourself."

"But she isn't you." Deidre crossed the room and wrapped her arms around her brother, giving him a quick squeeze. "I like having my whole family here."

"Yeah? When are Mom and Dad coming down?"

Deidre groaned. "Okay. Most of my family? All of my siblings?"

He smiled. "I'm still praying about it, okay? But if Anna gets in touch, don't discount her taking the job."

"Okay." Deidre tucked her hands in her pockets. "Whatever you decide, don't be a stranger. I like having you around."

He ruffled her hair and grinned. "The feeling's mutual, squirt. You're a lot less annoying now that you're grown up."

Laughing, Deidre shook her head. "Make sure you say goodbye to Claire. And let me know when you get back to D.C."

"Yes, Mom." Duncan took one last look at the room he'd occupied for the last month. Could he really go back to his desk job and deal with the annoyance of his new boss? Did he want to? *Jesus? What am I supposed to do?*

"McIntyre. My office. Now."

Duncan bit back a sigh. He'd been in the office exactly thirty minutes. It was just enough time to wade through the voicemails on his office phone and make notes. He had at least two hours of calls ahead of him. Dealing with his boss was low on the list of what he wanted to do. He grabbed a notepad and pen and pushed away from his desk.

His boss sat behind his obsessively clean desk, fingers steepled in front of him. "Nice of you to join us again."

Duncan managed a tight smile. He was not going to rise to the man's bait. He'd been on an approved leave. Paid, even. "It's good to be back."

"About that. Since you decided to desert us, I think it might be good for you to work closely with Evan going forward. That way, if you end up disappearing again the clients won't suffer."

"Sir. None of my clients suffered over the month I was gone. The two clients who were able to finalize their decisions while I was away were taken care of, by me, remotely. Work will start next week now that orders are starting to come in and crews have been scheduled. The other four clients that currently have active jobs are still considering their options and I checked in with them during my absence." Duncan clenched his pen and struggled to maintain a non-defensive posture.

"I see. So you're refusing to work with Evan?" His boss leaned forward, an almost gleeful smile on his face.

Duncan swallowed. The walls of whatever trap had been set were closing in. "Is partnering up a new policy for all employees? I don't recall seeing that email."

His lips thinned. "No. As yet it's not policy."

"Then I think I prefer to continue to work under the policies that were in place when I was hired, until such time as those policies change." Duncan cleared his throat and ignored his churning stomach. "Was there anything else?"

"Not as yet. No."

Duncan stood and forced himself to walk calmly from the office back to his cube. He set the notebook and pen down and picked up the phone. Knowing his boss, the man was watching him. So he'd act like everything was business as usual and not give him a chance to say something was amiss. He punched in the direct line for Mr. Marshall, Senior, and waited while it rang.

"Gerry Marshall."

"Hi, Mr. Marshall. It's Duncan McIntyre."

"Duncan, my boy. You're back?"

"Yes, sir."

"Good. Good. I've missed having you around. Everything okay?"

"Well, sir, I actually have a concern about a conversation I just had."

"Ken's pushing again, isn't he?"

"Yes, sir. He suggested that I needed to work in tandem with Evan for the foreseeable future."

"He didn't."

"He did, sir."

"And what did you say?"

Duncan rubbed the back of his neck. "I asked if it was policy to be doubled up. When he said no, I said I'd prefer to continue working according to the policies in place."

"Ha. I bet that put a twist in his shorts. Don't you worry, Duncan. You're one of the best we have on staff right now. And that Evan. Pfft. I've lost two long-time friends because of him. I managed to keep them as clients, but they hardly speak to me now. Not sure it was worth it, in all honesty. I'll handle Ken. You just keep doing your job. And let me know if there's any fallout."

"Yes, sir. Thank you." Duncan hung up the phone. He took a deep breath. Then another. Mr. Marshall, Senior, was great. But his son was old friends with his new boss, and he didn't for one minute believe that Junior would do anything other than what Ken recommended. Which meant that, despite Gerry's assurances, Duncan's job was in a precarious position.

Duncan stretched out on his couch and closed his eyes. His head throbbed. He'd had two more run-ins with Ken before the day was over. And one with Evan. He couldn't blame the kid—he was just doing with Ken told him. But it didn't fill him with a great desire to head back again in the morning. What was he doing here when he could be at Peacock Hill? Jeremiah had made it sound as if he turned away lots of landscape design business because he didn't feel qualified. Was that accurate or had he been exaggerating? Either way, did Duncan really want to set up his own shop?

A business owner. As a child, he'd watched his dad struggle. People made owning a small business look like the American dream. And yet...he'd seen first-hand there was so much more to it than doing what he loved. There was the constant scramble for business. There was paperwork. And taxes. And then, say he made a success of it and needed employees. That opened up another whole potential headache. More paperwork. And more taxes.

Was any of that worse than continuing to deal with Ken?

Duncan blew out a breath and reached for his phone. He needed Anna. Needed? His heart thumped steadily in his chest and he nodded. Needed. Preferably stretched out on the couch beside him. But since that wasn't a possibility, he could settle for hearing her voice.

"Hey there. I was just thinking of you."

Some of the stress of the day lifted at her greeting. "Yeah? Good things, I hope?"

"Always. How was your first day back to work?"

"Ugh. Let's talk about your day at work first."

She gave a sympathetic chuckle. "That bad? I'm sorry. Mine wasn't great. I don't think anyone actually answered the garden-oriented requests for the entire month of May. And I miss being outside. Today was such a pretty day here, and I was stuck inside. It didn't seem fair. But the other two reference librarians had a little party to welcome me back on Monday and there was still cake in the fridge."

"You got cake? Nice. I got called into Ken's office multiple times while he tried to saddle me with one of his cronies to watch over my shoulder. And I found out that one of my long-term clients passed away and his wife is selling their house and moving closer to their daughter."

"Aw. That's sad. Was he a believer?"

Duncan smiled. It was a good first question. "Yeah, he was. They went to the church we grew up in. Even though I don't go there anymore, they've always gone out of the way to stay in touch. And refer people with landscaping needs my way."

"That's good—makes it a little less sad. Everything okay with the boss?"

"I...don't know. I guess it's a matter of wait and see. I talked to Mr. Marshall, Senior. He's the only remaining brother of the original Marshall Brothers, and he's on my side. But his son, Mr. Marshall, Junior, is a friend of Ken and...I don't know how much pull either one of them has over the other. As much as I'd hate to lose my job, I have been praying for clear direction."

She snickered. "That would be pretty clear. Speaking of that...I had an idea. I was going to flesh it out a little more first before I talked to you about it, but I think maybe it's worth seeing if you're even remotely interested before I do."

She sounded so hesitant. It made him smile. He could picture her twisting her fingers together like he'd seen her do when she was nervous. "Yeah? Okay, hit me."

Anna cleared her throat. "So. Peacock Hill. We both know there'll be seasons when that's not really full-time work. And your sister talked about you taking on other jobs either through Jeremiah or from your own advertising."

"Right."

"What if you and I shared the job and went into business together?"

He scratched his chin as his thoughts jumbled together. That hadn't occurred to him. Why was that? A business partner could share the load where paperwork was concerned. And she had strengths that complemented his.

"You hate it. Forget I said anything."

"No. Wait. It's...interesting. There'd be a lot of details we'd need to work through." He sat up and sifted through the papers on his coffee table until he came up with an envelope from his water bill and a pen. He scribbled while he talked. "Would we need to form an official business? Some kind of LLC or something? And we'd need to make sure Deidre was okay with it. I'm not sure why she wouldn't be, but...we should double check. But first, we should figure out if there's really enough business to support both of us." He wasn't going to mention the possibility of them breaking up. But it was also a concern. What if that happened?

"Sure. Like I said, it's just the start of an idea. But maybe it's something to pray about?"

"Absolutely. In fact, why don't we do that now?" Duncan said a short prayer for guidance and clear assurance of God's will. Then they chatted a little longer before saying goodnight.

He tossed his phone on the coffee table and looked down at the list of questions he'd scribbled. Could they make a partnership like that work? Right now, his heart screamed that of course they could. And maybe their relationship was headed toward the marriage and family he kept imagining. But even that didn't mean they'd be able to find enough business to keep themselves afloat.

13

Anna rolled her chair over to the computer and logged in. She was alone at the desk. Fridays were usually slow, and she had the whole weekend off. She was even caught up on the backlog from her absence. It was sad that she'd been gone an entire month and only ended up with a day's worth of catch-up work. They didn't need her. Why did they keep her?

She wasn't complaining. Much. The job paid well and, on days like this, she could spend her time online doing her own research. Usually she took the time to work on school work. But since she'd taken the semester off—and, at the time, she hadn't known why, just simply that she should—she didn't have that hanging over her head. Which mean that, today, she'd be researching exactly what went into starting your own landscaping company with a business partner. Duncan had asked some good questions. The same ones had been in her own notes. So she'd start with those and go from there.

The phone on the desk rang. Anna hit enter on her first search and picked up the handset.

"Good afternoon. Archives reference, this is Anna."

"So official. It's Claire. McIntyre?"

Anna grinned. "Hi, Claire. What's up?"

"Nothing, really. I was just checking in, seeing how everything was going back in Richmond. Wondering if you'd heard from Duncan. That kind of thing."

"He's called every night. Hasn't he talked to you?" They'd seemed like they were close siblings—all three of them—why wouldn't Duncan have called?

"Oh, sure. Not every night though." There was laughter in Claire's voice. "So things are still good?"

After just one week apart, they'd better be. Otherwise they had no business dating in the first place. "Yeah. Why?"

"Well...I had this idea. Deidre thought it was amazing and wondered why no one came up with it before and has been nagging me about mentioning it for two days. Of course, I chickened out when I talked to Duncan. He sounded so down about how things are going at his job, I didn't want to suggest something if it ended up not being a good idea."

"All right?"

"Here's the thing. What if you and Duncan went into business together and shared the job at Peacock Hill?"

Anna burst into laughter.

"No. I really think it could work. Let me explain what I was thinking."

"Claire, I wasn't laughing because I thought it was a bad idea. I was laughing because I'm sitting here researching exactly what it would take to do just that."

Anna sighed. "Duncan...isn't sure. He didn't nix the idea immediately, but he wasn't as excited about it as I'd hoped. I'm trying to believe it's because he's one of those people who has to check every box before he'll step out."

"Hmm. Yeah, that probably summarizes Duncan well enough. He's a planner."

Anna nodded. That was what she remembered from college. And success at a place like Marshall Brothers likely needed that as a trait. But what did it mean for their relationship? At thirty-two, she was ready to be married and start a family. She'd always wanted to be a young mom. At this point, that ship had sailed. But she'd really like to avoid being an old one. "Okay. I'll go with that and do some research and write it up more clearly for him. You really think it's a workable idea?"

"I do. And so does Deidre. In fact, she's positively giddy about it. Of course, she has you and Duncan married off. Her relationship with Jeremiah has her seeing everyone as happily paired off as she is."

"Yeah? Like you and Danny?" Anna bit her lip. Was that too much? She and Claire had gotten along, but they hadn't spent so much time together that Anna had an idea about how Claire would handle teasing.

Claire's sigh was loud in Anna's ear. "Not you, too. We're friends."

"Uh-huh. Got it. Even though he's hot?"

"Why are you noticing that he's hot? You have Duncan. And Danny's too young for you anyway."

"Ouch. I'm only like four years older than him. That's not exactly cougar material." Anna opened a link from her search results in a new tab.

"If I admit that, yes, I think he's hot, will you leave it alone?"

"Sure. Though I will state, for the record, that I think the two of you look good together." Anna typed in another search and started scrolling through the results, opening the ones that sounded promising.

"Yeah, well. He treats me like I'm his little sister. So I don't think anything's going to develop there. Even if I wanted it to."

"Don't you?"

"I don't know. Maybe. But it takes more than one person wanting it to make it happen. Anyway, between you and Duncan and Deidre and Jeremiah, I should be able to play doting aunt before too long. That's almost as good."

Heat burned Anna's cheeks. "You really think so?"

"I've never seen him act like he does around you. So, yeah. I do. You're good for him. It's a bonus that I like you."

"I like you, too. If you have any suggestions for figuring out the legal ins and outs of setting up our own business, I'm open to pointers."

"Ha. Do I ever? Give me your email address and I'll shoot some info your way."

Anna rattled it off. Claire had run the business side of Deidre's handyman operation in Northern

Virginia. Before Deidre closed it down to focus on Peacock Hill. Getting information from someone who was in the know like that was always better than trying to figure it out from scratch. "Thanks, Claire."

"Don't mention it. Any chance of you coming down this weekend?"

She'd like to. She missed the mountains. And Claire and Deidre. But... "Probably not. I'm not sure when I'll get back there, honestly. If Duncan can make it down here next weekend, well, I'd rather stay put."

Claire laughed. "All right. Just know the door's always open. Take care."

Anna hung up the phone and logged into her email. While she waited for Claire to get her the information, she scrolled through some of the links she'd opened and took notes. There were hoops to jump through, which wasn't surprising. But it didn't look too hard. Or too overwhelming.

The hardest part might just be convincing Duncan to do it.

Stomach churning, Anna dialed Duncan's cell and waited while it rang.

"Hey. This is a nice surprise."

"Do you have a minute? I know you're at work."

"I always have a minute for you. What's up?"

"I talked to Claire on Friday and she sent me some information. I spent the weekend putting together...I guess you'd call it a business plan. I wondered if you'd like to see it." She held her breath, waiting for his answer.

"Definitely. Can you email it to my personal account?"

"Done." Anna clicked send on the email she'd already composed and pressed a hand to her stomach. That hadn't been hard. Why had it seemed like it was going to? "If you have ideas or thoughts or questions or...whatever, just put them in and send it back. Okay?"

"Sounds good. Oops. I have to run. Love you."

The phone clicked. Anna stared, wide-eyed, at her phone. Love you? Her heart hammered in her chest. Was that a mistake or did he mean it? She...was in love with him. But she hadn't expected that he would feel the same so quickly. Maybe his talk about having a crush on her in college hadn't been exaggerated.

"Are you done with the computer? There's a man at the desk with gardening questions." Roberta, the older of the two other reference librarians, nodded toward a man waiting at the front of the desk.

"Sure." Anna logged out of the computer and pushed thoughts of loving Duncan out of her mind. Or tried to. She missed him. It was a quiet ache in her heart every day. Talking on the phone wasn't quite the same thing. And that wasn't productive right now, either. She fixed a smile on her face and approached the waiting man. "Hi, I'm Anna. I'm told you need some help with garden-related information?"

"Sure do. I'm Wade. My wife's got it in her head that she'd like a sort of mini-version of a formal English garden in the backyard now that the kids are grown. I'm not sure what that even means, to be honest, so I figured the best place to find out something about a historic garden would be here."

That wasn't completely accurate, but Anna could work with it. Did they not have the Internet though? The man was older—maybe her parents' age—but still young enough to have learned to use e-mail and a web browser. "I'm sure I can help you. Did you have any general ideas beyond 'English garden' that you wanted to go off of?"

He shrugged, his gaze steadily holding hers. "Not really. She saw a program on TV about Bronze Age mansions here in the U.S. and got the idea from it."

Bronze Age? Her history was rusty, but hadn't that been before the Roman Empire? And in Mesopotamia? English gardens were definitely not a thing yet. She chewed her lip. "Could she have meant Gilded Age? The early nineteen hundreds here in the U.S.?"

"That's it. That's the one. Knew bronze sounded wrong but couldn't think of anything better." He grinned. "I can see why you work here."

She smiled even as her heart fell. Sure, she was good at her job. And it was nice when people noticed. But she didn't want to be stuck here forever showing people books and photos of gardens when she could be designing and planting them. "Let's go browse the stacks.

I know a couple of books off the top of my head that'll give you a nudge in the right direction as far as layout and the types of plants that will do well in Virginia while still maintaining the look and feel you're going for."

"Sounds good."

Anna flipped up the pass-through in the counter and walked past him into the tall shelves of the archives. She'd spent enough time poking through the reference books when Deidre had first contacted her that she didn't even need to look up the call letters. "Here we are. There's a lovely home here in Richmond called Maymont. It's open to the public, so if you want, you can visit and see these types of gardens in action. They're featured in this book, along with several other of the mansions found on the East coast. And this one has some good close-ups of English gardens as well. Why don't you get started with those and if you need more, come find me?"

"Okay." Wade patted his pockets and offered a sheepish grin. "I don't suppose you have some paper I could use?"

"Of course. Here." Anna set the books down on an empty table. "I'll be right back."

Who came to the library—the *archives* and reference section of the library—without paper and a pencil? Didn't everyone know these materials couldn't be removed? She yanked open a drawer behind the desk and grabbed a pad of lined yellow paper and took two short pencils from the cup on the counter. After a moment's thought, she grabbed a ruler. If she were the one drawing garden plans, she'd need a straight edge.

"Here you go. I thought the ruler might come in handy if you decide to make any sketches. I'll be at the desk if you need anything else."

"Thanks so much." The man smiled and looked back down at the books.

Anna shook her head and went back to the desk. The glorious job of the reference librarian—looking stuff up for people who couldn't manage to do it themselves. Which was unfair. Often, people had tried. But this guy? He didn't seem to be all that motivated when it came to the gardens. Then again, if it was his wife's honey-do and not something he wanted to do, why would he be?

She picked up a stack of books someone had left on the counter and checked the backs. Might as well get them back on the shelves. Then she could look in on Wade and see if he needed anything more. If she knew—really knew—that she and Duncan were going to be setting out their shingle, she'd mention their new business to him. After the last month, Anna had a pretty good feel for English gardens, so they could definitely take him on as a client. But it was too new an idea to do that. And she certainly didn't want anyone at the archives to overhear her. They frowned on moonlighting.

When the last book was back where it belonged, she angled toward the table where she'd left Wade. It had been twenty minutes. That ought to be long enough for him to know if he needed something else.

Wade was in the process of tearing a few sheets of paper off the notepad.

"So, what do you think? Did you find what you needed?"

He jumped and chuckled. "I think so. Got the layout and the gist of the types of plants to look for. Still don't understand why someone would want such a thing, but...I do love my wife."

She smiled. That was sweet. "That's a good thing. Have you been married long?"

"Coming up on forty years. We have three great kids, all grown now, and out of the house. But they keep in touch, which is a blessing. You married?"

"No, sir, not yet."

"Hope to be then, someday?"

"I do. When I find the man God has for me." Maybe that would be the end of that conversation. Usually strangers didn't like it when you brought up God. And it was downright odd to be talking about this with someone she'd just met.

His eyes gleamed. "Aha. That right there's the secret to a long marriage. God. You keep Him front and center, everything else will fall into place. Got a fella?"

A fella? Wade wasn't old enough to talk like that, but it still somehow managed to fit. Anna found herself nodding. "I do. He's great. But he's not local, so...it's complicated."

"Hmm. But he's a good guy? Godly?"

"Absolutely."

"Then you just keep praying and I'm confident God will make a way for you and Duncan to be together." Wade folded the papers in half before waving them. "Thanks for this. Appreciate your help. Have a great day now."

"You too." Anna watched as he walked away, then frowned. Duncan. She hadn't said Duncan's name, had she? She closed her eyes and tried to replay the conversation. Maybe she had. His name was always on the tip of her tongue. But...she couldn't remember doing it. She sighed and picked up the two books she'd pulled down for Wade and took them back to their shelf. Whether she had or hadn't mentioned Duncan's name, there was nothing to do about it now. She'd just keep an eye out and see if she spotted Wade—or anyone— hanging around.

14

Duncan toed off his shoes and closed the door behind him before calling out. "Mom? Dad? I'm here."

"I'm in the kitchen." His mom's voice carried down the hallway and he grinned.

He sniffed. Mom made pot roast? He followed the scent back to the kitchen and smiled. "Smells good. Kind of fancy for a Monday night."

"Never too fancy for my boy." She grinned and leaned over to kiss his cheek. "I'm glad you could make it. How was work today?"

"Eh. I survived to try another day. I think right now that's the best I can expect." Duncan snuck a carrot off the platter where his mother was arranging the roast. It burned his fingers but the taste was worth it. "Yum."

"Did you wash those fingers? Keep them out of my food." She winked and spooned the last of the vegetables around the meat. "Your father was supposed to be setting the table. Can you go check on him?"

Duncan glanced over at the kitchen table. "We're not eating in here?"

"No. I thought it'd be fun to use the dining room since it's more than just me and Dad." She pushed a bowl of salad toward him. "Take this with you."

He grabbed the bowl and passed through the door into the dining room. His father was seated at his usual spot, scrolling on his phone.

He glanced up when Duncan entered. "Hey, Dunc. Glad you could join us. It got your mom to make pot roast. On a week-night. You need to come over more often while you're in town."

While he was in town? What did that mean? "You know I enjoy hanging out with you guys. It's just a bit of a drive. But I'll see what I can do."

"Go see if your mother has more she needs you to help with so we can eat." His dad grinned and turned back to his phone.

His mother came in, her arms laden with the pot roast platter and another bowl. "Wade, put that phone away."

Flushing guiltily, he hit a button on the side of his phone and tucked it into his shirt pocket. "All better. That smells fantastic, honey."

"Thanks. Duncan you have a seat and pour yourself a glass of iced tea. I made it the way you like."

"Yeah?" His mom made the best sweet tea. She didn't do it often, because his dad bordered on diabetes. So it was a treat, for sure. He poured himself a glass and passed the pitcher to his dad who waved it away.

"I have water. But thanks. You can send some roast this way though."

"Wade. Why don't you say grace before we dish up?" His mother pulled out her chair and sat.

Duncan bowed his head as his father said a brief and to the point prayer. When he'd said amen, he reached for the roast and speared several slices along with a generous helping of potatoes and carrots before passing the platter to his dad.

His dad took the platter. "Thanks. I met your young lady today. Seems like a sweet girl."

"Wait, what? You met Anna? How? Where? Why didn't she call me?" Was she in town? Why would she come up and not let him know?

His dad grinned and pointed his fork at his mom. "Told you she didn't know who I was."

"And I still think it's rude. Plus, now you're on the hook for that garden project."

Duncan looked between his parents. "Would someone please tell me what's going on? Is Anna here?"

"No, no. I drove down to Richmond today and stopped by the archives. Made up some story about your mother wanting a formal English garden in the back yard. Anyway, she helped me with a few books and was very considerate. And when I asked about you, she turned a very pretty shade of pink and commented that she was waiting for the man God has for her. I like her. A lot."

Duncan's mind was spinning. "Why were you in Richmond?"

"To meet Anna. I told you that." He shook his head at his wife. "It's like he doesn't listen."

"Wade, stop teasing the boy. Honey, your father's been curious for six weeks now about this girl. Deidre gives us some information, but we've heard nothing from you. So he decided to take matters into his own hands. I have to say, from the photo he took, that she's a real pretty little thing."

"You drove two hours to Richmond with a fake story so you could meet Anna. Is that right?"

His dad nodded. "About. You know I like to drive. And, as it turns out, now that she's seen the drawing I made, your mother actually *does* want an English formal garden. So I have a new project."

"I can design you a garden. What did Anna say?"

"What do you mean?"

"When you told her you were my dad?"

"Oh. I didn't." His dad cut a chunk of his roast and popped it in his mouth. "Didn't see the need."

Duncan closed his eyes. Now what was he supposed to do? "Great. That's...great."

"Oh, it's not so bad." His mom pushed the bowl of salad toward him. "Eat some vegetables, too."

"Carrots and potatoes are vegetables." But he put a small helping of salad on his plate. It never paid to argue with Mom. She'd end up getting her way in the end. She always did. "What did she say about me, exactly?"

His dad chuckled and repeated the conversation. "That's as good as I can remember. Like I said, she sounds a lot like a woman in love. Or right on the cusp of it."

In love. His words the other night came back to him and his neck heated. She hadn't said anything about it in any of their subsequent phone calls. Maybe she hadn't heard him. It certainly wasn't the way he'd meant to tell her. And it was still probably too soon. But it also felt right.

"No witty response?" His mother smiled and served herself more salad. "Hmm."

"I'm not sure what to say. You guys know I've had a crush on her since college." Duncan shrugged.

His dad nodded. "That's what I thought. And one of the reasons I wanted to meet her. For what it's worth, I like her."

"Yeah? Me, too." Duncan mashed one of the little potatoes and scooted it into the puddle of jus from his roast. "So, if you'll drive all that way to spy on Anna, when are you going to go see Peacock Hill?"

His mom laughed. "That's the same question I asked. We're thinking maybe next weekend. Rumor has it you might be out of town then, too."

Duncan's heart sped up. A chance to see Anna again. To hold her. Yeah. He needed that. He nodded. "That's the plan."

Duncan hooked his phone to the car's built-in system and dialed Anna as he backed out of his parents'

driveway. Dinner had been nice. Except that it had left him missing Anna more than ever. He needed to at least hear her voice.

"Hi there. You're earlier than usual."

Duncan checked the time on the car's dash. "Am I? Too early?"

"Nope. Just surprised. How was your day?"

He chuckled. "It's getting better, now that I'm talking to you. I haven't had a chance to look at the business plan yet. I thought I'd do that when I got home."

"You're not home yet?"

"No. My mom called and invited me to dinner. So I'm just leaving their neighborhood. I went straight there from the office. How was your day?"

"Good. Mostly. Though I had a weird customer." Anna described her interactions with Wade. "But he seemed nice. So unless he shows up again, I'm not going to worry about it."

Duncan chuckled. "You'll probably meet him again. That was my dad. He got tired of waiting for me to introduce you and decided to take matters into his own hands. I'm sorry if he worried you."

She laughed. "Really? That actually makes me feel better. At the end, he said your name and I've been second-guessing myself all afternoon, because I didn't remember mentioning you by name. So I kept wondering if he was a creepy stalker or maybe I was losing my mind."

"Yeah. He probably thought he was being cute. He doesn't think things through all the time. But he means well."

"I liked him. Until I got worried. So now I can push the worry out and just like him. And I like that he came all that way just to meet me."

Duncan let himself relax. At least she wasn't upset. "He liked you, too."

Anna chatted cheerfully about her day while he navigated through the constant traffic of the D.C. area. He didn't love this place. He was only here because it's where he'd grown up and he'd wanted to be near family. And Marshall Brothers was here. Straight out of college, a job with them had seemed like the pinnacle of everything he'd been working for. He'd never dreamed of having his own firm like so many of his classmates did. But the idea was growing on him.

Anna cleared her throat. "So. Can I ask you a question?"

Duncan turned into his apartment's parking garage. "Of course."

"The other night. Friday? You said something and I wanted to ask you about that."

Friday. When he'd said "love you." He swallowed and punched a button on the phone to detach it from the car as he parked. "Yeah?"

"Did you mean it?"

He pressed the button for the elevator. "I did. I...on the phone wasn't how I wanted to do this, but I love you, Anna."

"I love you, too."

Grinning, Duncan stepped into the elevator. "If I lose you in the elevator, I'll call you right back, okay?"

"Okay."

Sure enough, as soon as the doors slid closed, the call disconnected. Duncan pressed his floor. She loved him. Did life get any better than that?

Duncan kicked his shoes off and loosened his tie. What a day. Ken was doing his best to make it impossible for him to stay. There was no possible other explanation for the work that was getting shifted his way. And he couldn't go running to Mr. Marshall every time there was a problem. That was a sure way to wear out his welcome.

He'd spent last night talking with Anna about the business plan she'd put together. He had to admit, it was tempting. He hadn't been able to get it out of his mind all day. He padded to his bedroom and hung up his work clothes, changing into pajama pants and a t-shirt. He'd toss some of the leftovers his mom sent home with him last night into the microwave and spend some more time looking over that proposal. There was a lot of risk, but the potential was also huge. Could he really do it? Ditch Marshall Brothers and start fresh like that? With Anna.

Anna. Working with her every day? That could be amazing. Or terrible. What if, after working with him, she decided she didn't actually love him? Or went back to thinking that he didn't appreciate her ideas? She'd seemed to get past that quickly enough at Peacock Hill...but he hadn't had much cause to challenge any of her ideas. What would happen if he did?

With his plate in hand, Duncan settled on the couch and flipped open the printouts he'd made of the business plan. He'd made notes in the margin in several places with ideas and suggestions. Maybe...would talking to her about those give him a glimpse at how she'd respond? It was better to find out now, before he staked everything on the possibility. He picked up his cell and punched Anna's number.

"Hey, you."

Duncan smiled, his heart warming at the sound of her voice. "Hey. How was your day?"

"Oh, you know. Same old. What about you?"

"That probably sums it up. Though I got a couple of photos of the gardens from Deidre. Some of the plants are starting to bloom. Did you get them?"

"I did. It's nice to see how it's looking. I'm a little worried the nook with the two-person bench in the picture garden isn't going to have enough color. Maybe she should add in some tulips and maybe a bush with variegated leaves—something to add interest."

Duncan considered. That photo had been the least impressive. And yet, sometimes simple was good. "What if we got two more urns and set them on either side of the bench? Then, anyone taking photos would have a place for customized arrangements like they do in the chapel garden. That'd be a lovely spot for some bride and groom pictures, just the two of them. Or bride and her mom."

There was a slight pause. "That's a good idea. Do you want to tell her?"

"I can. Or you can. Doesn't matter. Do you have a preference?"

"I'll do it. You don't mind?"

"Nope." Duncan cleared his throat. "I've been looking at the business plan and have a few questions and suggestions. Do you want to talk them over on the phone or should I send them to you in an email?"

"Are they major?"

What constituted major? A couple of them were a suggestion to look at things from a different angle, but it didn't take away the idea at all. It just tweaked it. "Um. Maybe?"

"It might be easier to send them and then we can talk them over this weekend? You're still planning to come down, right?"

The breathless anticipation in her voice eased the tightening in his chest. She didn't sound thrilled that he had questions. At least she was still excited about seeing him. "Right. I found a hotel near your apartment that wasn't too bad."

"I'm sorry I couldn't find anyone who could put you up. Other than my neighbor, Sean, I don't have any guy friends, apparently. And he totally would've done it, but he's got two weddings this weekend and wouldn't be around. He said it'd be weird to have someone staying at his place without being able to be a good host."

"I get that. When you come up here, I figured you could stay with my folks. I don't really know anyone to ask about that myself." He did have a pull-out sofa, but that seemed like a bad idea all around. Having her stay the night was asking for temptation at the best and giving his neighbors the completely wrong idea at the worst. Since he'd tried, subtly, to be a witness to the people in his building, he really didn't need to undo that. Not even if he was pretty sure neither he nor Anna would let something happen.

"Yeah? I'd like that. Your dad was nice and I know I'd enjoy meeting your mom."

"Do you want to come up here instead of me coming down?"

"Maybe next weekend? I had a few activities already planned for us."

"Sounds good. I figured I'd just drive down Saturday morning. If I get up and get going, I should still be to your place by nine. Maybe nine-thirty."

"Even if it's ten, that's fine. There's no point in dealing with Friday traffic if you don't have to."

He chuckled. "Well. I have to admit I'd like a chance to see you one day sooner. But...it still makes more sense to wait."

"I miss you. More than I thought possible."

"Yeah? I know how that feels." The buzzer for his door sounded. "Hey, someone's at my door. I'll email you the business plan stuff later tonight and we can plan to talk it over this weekend. Okay?"

"Sure. If you want to call back later, you can."

He smiled. "I might do that. I love you."

"Love you, too."

Duncan hit end and looked through the peep hole in his door before grinning and unlocking the door. "Hey, man. What are you doing here?"

"I was in the building tuning a piano, thought I'd see if you were home. I heard a rumor you'd been out of town all month."

"In May, yeah. Come in. It's good to see you, Nick."

Nick stepped in with a smile and set his toolbox down by the door. "But you're back now, for good?"

Duncan shrugged and closed the door. "I'm not sure, actually. Can I get you a drink? I've got some soda and maybe enough iced tea to wet your whistle."

"Soda's good. Unless it's diet."

"I have not recently become a woman, so no, it's not diet." Duncan shook his head and grabbed two cans from the fridge, motioning Nick to take a seat in the living room.

Nick laughed. "Just checking."

Duncan handed Nick his soda before flopping into a chair and putting his feet on the coffee table. "You need to stop by more often. It's been what, six months?"

"Every time I come to tune the piano in apartment 6C, yeah."

"You don't actually have to be in the building tuning to come over, you know." Duncan grinned.

"That goes both ways. Although I guess you get a pass if you're out of town. What were you up to?" Nick popped the top and took a long drink.

"I'm guessing my mom is your source?"

Nick grinned.

"She didn't mention Deidre bought a big old house in southwest Virginia?"

"Yeah? That's cool. Why?"

Duncan chuckled. "You know Dee, she's fixing it up. Of course, this time she plans to stay and turn it into some kind of retreat center and wedding venue. The building and grounds work for that, no question. I just wonder if she's really going to enjoy not having more projects than fixing something when it leaks."

"Which'll never happen if she's doing the reno work."

"Right?" Duncan shook his head. "Anyway, I went down to help get the grounds back in shape."

"And it's true she's marrying a handyman from down there?" Nick fiddled with the top of his soda can.

"Dude. Please tell me you don't still have a thing for my sister."

Nick lifted a shoulder. "I wouldn't call it a thing. Just...an interest. She's a great girl."

Duncan couldn't argue with that, Deidre was a good catch. But he liked Jeremiah. And as far as he'd ever been able to tell, his sister had never returned any of the interest Nick showed. "Well, they're not officially engaged yet. But he's bought a ring—he showed it to me—I'm not sure when he'll give it to her though."

"Ah well. She never seemed all that interested in more than friendship anyway." Nick sighed. "I'll just have to content myself with living vicariously through Piero's misadventures in the dating world."

Duncan started to laugh and had to cover his mouth to keep his soda from spraying everywhere. "Your brother...I've never met twins as different as you two."

"That's because we're fraternal. And half-Italian." Nick pulled a tissue from the box on the coffee table and offered it to Duncan. "Or so my mama always said."

"Met any new celebrities that you need to tell me about?"

Nick shook his head. "They've been scheduling me in the morning at the Kennedy Center, long before any performers show up. I can't complain. It leaves more time for private tuning jobs. And I'm teaching a few lessons, too."

"Piano lessons? Really?"

"Gotta make a living, right? I played an offertory at church, next thing I know I've got the office calling me asking if they can give out my number to the moms who keep asking for it because they want to know if I teach lessons. And okay, I never finished my bachelor's degree in piano pedagogy, but I know enough to teach beginners."

"Understatement. I'll still never forget the part of the piece you were writing you played after that one men's group."

Nick's face flamed. "No one was supposed to be there. The notes just came while the speaker was going, I knew I needed to play it before I got home or it'd evaporate."

"You've got talent, man. Why aren't you doing something with it?"

"To *you* it's talent. To the music world?" Nick shrugged. "It's just a hobby. Certainly nothing that's going to keep me in tacos."

Duncan laughed. "When's the last time you ate a taco? I thought you were allergic to them, or some such nonsense."

"Fine, fine. Lasagna. Except it takes too long to make if you do it right, and I can't abide the store bought. At least with a taco, it's not supposed to be some kind of amazing culinary treat."

"You're just not eating the right tacos."

Nick furrowed his brow. "This from the man who doesn't eat nachos."

Duncan smiled. "I'm actually a recent nacho convert. Jeremiah—my soon-to-be brother-in-law— makes some pretty darn good ones."

"That's just mean. You know I'll never manage to top that. The one time I made your sister Italian food, she was all about how oregano gave her hives. I guess we weren't meant to be."

"Sorry."

"No you aren't. I can see on your face that you like Jeremiah. Although, who names their kid Jeremiah in today's world?"

"Really, Nicolo? With the fancy little slash over top of the last o and everything? You're going to make fun of someone's name?" Duncan drained the rest of his soda.

"Why are we friends again? You're like four years older than I am and mean." Nick set his soda aside and started to stand.

"Oh, sit down. You know I'm razzing you. And we're friends because you've been tuning my mom's piano for five years and hitting on my sister for about that long. It was either get to be friends or beat you up. Friends just seemed easier."

Nick chuckled and sat. "I wasn't really going to leave. I figure I wait long enough, I can talk you into ordering pizza and paying for the pie."

"Conniving." Duncan slid his phone out of his pocket and pulled up the website for the only pizza place Nick would deign to eat from. "You're still okay with Italianio's, right? Even though it can't compare to your brother Marco's pizza and blah blah blah?"

"Get the Italian sausage on it. You'll thank me later."

"Cannoli?"

"Is my last name Carter?"

Duncan laughed and punched in the order. "Done. Forty-five minutes or thereabout. I'll admit I was skeptical when you first mentioned them, but you're right, the wait's worth it. Those cannoli."

"Yeah. Oh yeah." Nick patted his stomach. "What's going on at work?"

Duncan drummed his fingers on his leg. Nick had already made a few comments about cobbling together a living. And yet, he'd been doing it for several years now—successfully. Maybe getting a different perspective than the one he'd formed watching his dad was warranted. "You own your own business. Can I ask you some questions?"

15

Anna paced from one end of her tiny living room to the other. Duncan should be here soon. She looked around, checking for any stray clutter. It was her biggest fight—keeping the piles at bay. Her mother had chided her constantly about her bedroom growing up, and had smirked—kindly, but still a smirk—the first time she and Dad had visited her apartment. Now that they lived in California, they didn't get to see the improvement she'd made. Maybe if things continued to go well with Duncan they'd have a reason to at least visit. Her brother, his wife, and their four kids had been a compelling reason to move across the country. Anna couldn't deny that. But she also couldn't help feeling a little abandoned.

She jolted at the knock on her door and pressed a hand to her stomach. That had to be him. And there weren't any visible piles unless he went into her bedroom. Which he wouldn't be doing. Anna grabbed the door and pulled it open with a grin. "You're here."

Duncan laughed and opened his arms. "I am. Took a little longer than I thought, sorry."

Anna stepped into his embrace, lifting her face. "I'm just glad you made it."

He lowered his lips to hers and everything around them faded away. It was like being swept off to a deserted island where only the two of them existed. When he eased back, he smiled. "Hi."

"Come on in. Do you want some coffee or anything?" Anna stepped into the living room and clasped her fingers together. Why was her heart racing like this? She'd had people over before. Even guys she'd dated. But with Duncan it seemed...more important.

"Sure. Coffee's never a bad idea. Can I use your bathroom?"

"Oh. Of course. Down the hall on the right." Anna pointed. When he'd started down that way, she went to the kitchen and poured two mugs of coffee. Not that she needed any extra caffeine in her system right now. But holding the drink would give her something to do. If only it would guarantee she wouldn't make a fool out of herself. Seeing him again after two weeks...it was almost like starting over. Except it wasn't. She'd told him she loved him. Standing in front of him drove it home.

She carried the coffees into the living room and set them on the little end table. She didn't have a coffee table. She'd had one when she first moved in, but it was always a pile collector. So she'd finally gotten rid of it. Same with her kitchen table, opting instead to eat at the little counter ledge that jutted out. The fewer places she had to collect things, the better.

Duncan sat next to her and reached for the coffee. He took a long sip. "Perfect. Thanks. So. What did you want to do first?"

Kissing him again was at the top of that list. But it was something that should wait until they weren't alone in her apartment. So. Second on the list. She checked the time on the clock hanging on the wall. "Maymont won't be open for another hour, at least. Why don't we look over the business plan for a bit?"

"Okay." He drew his phone out of his pocket, turned it sideways, and tapped the screen. Then he stopped and took her hand. "Why don't we pray first?"

Anna nodded and closed her eyes.

"Dear Jesus, please be with Anna and me as we talk about this possible business venture. Help us to know Your will—whether this is what You would have us do and, if so, how You want us to do it. Be with us today. Help us to glorify You with our relationship. Amen." Duncan squeezed her hand and let go so he could pick up his phone again. "Did you look at the suggestions I sent you?"

"Yeah. Hang on, I have a printout we can work from." She rose and crossed to her desk. Since she'd spent the bulk of her time last night organizing it, the business plan came easily to hand in its cheerful purple folder. "Here we are. I went ahead and printed the one you sent, with your notes intact. I thought it would make it easier to discuss."

He grinned and pecked her cheek. "Good thinking. So...start at the beginning, I guess?"

Anna nodded. He seemed hesitant—as if he was scared to talk through the thoughts and changes he'd mentioned. But they'd all been good, and even if she wasn't thrilled with one or two, she could see why he would have come up with them. There was room for expansion and improvement. After all, she'd thrown the document together over a weekend. She'd been more in a hurry to have something to prove to him it was a valid idea than to have it perfect right off the mark.

Over the next hour, they worked through the pages one at a time. Anna made notes in the margins as they hammered out decisions. All in all, it had been relatively painless. Duncan listened when she talked and didn't seem as eager to override her as he'd been in college. Hopefully that would be something that continued. He'd been like that at Peacock Hill, too. So either he'd had a change of heart or...could she have been wrong all along? That was something to mull over another time.

Anna flipped the last page over and sighed. "Done."

"Yeah. It's like having homework all over again."

She laughed. "Just like. I can make corrections and send you the new document—maybe tomorrow after you leave?"

"Sure. That works. I'm still...not one hundred percent sure that this is the right thing, but it looks better and better every day I spend back at Marshall Brothers."

Anna reached over and squeezed his hand. She would've walked away long before now, from the things Duncan had told her about his boss. "I can give my notice any time. Just let me know. Now...want to go wander the gardens at Maymont?"

"With you? Absolutely. And I'm under strict instructions by Deidre to tour the house as well. She said she needs some ideas for what to do about the music room. It had silk wallpaper that has mold and is shredding in some places. So it obviously can't be repaired but she's not sure replacing is the right plan either. She thought maybe Maymont, since it's the same era, would have some other wall treatments that might work."

Wall treatments. That was far outside her comfort zone. But since she hadn't actually been through the house, despite visiting the estate multiple times a year for the last eight years that she'd lived in Richmond, it seemed like a reasonable enough addition to their excursion. "Okay. Let's go."

Duncan slipped his hand in hers. She looked down at their clasped fingers and smiled. Life couldn't get better than this.

Anna kicked off her shoes and danced into the kitchen. What a glorious day. She laughed and spun in a circle before reaching for the fridge door and looking inside. Aha. She'd made lemonade...when had she made that? She opened the lid and sniffed. It smelled okay. Could lemonade go bad? Especially if it was made from a fine powder that you added water to?

With a shrug, she poured the last of it into a glass and tasted. Seemed normal. She put the pitcher in the sink and carried her drink to the living room. She'd read for an hour and then go to bed. Duncan was going to pick her up for church at nine, so she had plenty of time in the morning to get ready. Which meant she didn't need to rush to bed, even if it was nearly ten.

Her phone chimed with an incoming text.

"How'd it go?"

She frowned at the number. Who was...Deidre. She shook her head and hit dial.

"Hello?" Deidre picked up on the first ring.

"Didn't you tell me you don't text?"

"Jeremiah's working on me. But this is better. How'd it go?"

Anna sipped the juice and set it on the floor next to the couch. She wiggled to get comfortable and sighed. "It was good. Though I'm curious how you know I'm home."

"Duncan texted me the pictures he took at Maymont. I figured he probably wasn't doing that if he was still with you. 'Cause if he'd been going to do it while you were around, it would've been earlier in the day."

"That's some pretty solid, logical thinking."

Deidre snorted. "What's that supposed to mean?"

Anna grinned. "Nothing. Just an observation."

"Uh-huh. Right. Did you talk to him about the business plan? Claire told me it looks solid."

Anna glanced at the purple folder, also on the floor. "We did. He had some questions that we worked through. And he's still hesitant. But I think it's looking possible."

"Yay! Maybe I should get Dad to give him the 'Be your own man' speech."

Anna snickered. "What's that?"

"Basically, exactly what it sounds like. It's Dad's version of a small business owner pep talk. 'Cause he firmly believes that everyone should own and run a business at some point in their life, if only so they understand and respect people who do it for a living."

"Ha. Sounds like my parents' 'Work in the service industry' speech." Anna shook her head and took another sip of lemonade. How many times had she listened to that speech in high school and college? She'd never followed the advice, but she did try to keep it in mind when she ate out or dealt with people who did work there. Basic courtesy was really just part of trying to be salt and light, anyway. If a person was nasty to people they considered beneath them, how could they could have any witness for Jesus?

"So is 'good' all I'm getting out of you about this entire day-long date? 'Cause that's really lame."

"I'm sorry. I'm a little out of practice with the whole spill all the details to your best girlfriend thing." Since she hadn't had a best girlfriend since...ever? "What, specifically, do you need to know?"

"Seriously? Let's start with something simple. Did he pray with you?"

Anna grinned. That had been a pleasant surprise. "Several times. It was nice."

"Good for him. Mom would be proud. Not that I'm telling Mom, mind you. But that was something she always harped on as well—that we should only marry someone we could pray with. Someone we'd been able to pray with from the beginning."

Marry? Anna's heart began to race. "Um. No one said anything about marriage."

"Well, not yet. But...I thought you were in love with him?" The disappointment and confusion was obvious in Deidre's voice.

"I am. It's just a big leap to move from love straight to marriage." Wasn't it? Sure, she'd had the odd fantasy. She was human. And female. And Duncan was...amazing. But there was a whole progression of things that had to happen first, wasn't there? Anna wiped suddenly damp palms on her legs. Was that where Duncan's mind was? "I'm not saying it's not a possibility down the road."

"You're what, thirty-two?"

"Yeah?"

"Don't you want babies?"

This conversation was getting a little odd. She liked Deidre. Considered her a friend, even. But... "I guess so. But people are having babies in their forties these days."

"Pfft. Only with medical intervention."

Anna frowned. Was that true? Celebrities seemed to pop out babies well into their forties—she'd just assumed that was the case for regular people as well.

"I'm not saying it can't happen. Look at Abraham and Sarah, right?" Deidre laughed. "But I am saying, if you love my brother and he loves you...don't leave him hanging."

A whisper of a quote from some costumed drama her mother had forced her to watch flitted through her brain, but she couldn't quite catch it. Even still, maybe it wasn't bad advice. She wanted to be a younger, fun parent. Maybe younger was slipping away faster than she'd anticipated. "I won't. But I'm not proposing to him just to keep on your timeline."

Deidre chuckled. "That's fair. I'm glad you had a good time."

"I really did."

"Then I'm happy. Good night."

Anna ended the call and flopped back on the couch. Marriage. Was Duncan already thinking that way? Was that why Deidre had mentioned it? Her phone buzzed with another text. This one from Duncan and it said simply, "I love you."

She smiled and her whole body warmed as she typed back, "I love you too. Lots."

Anna tucked her arm through Duncan's as they stood for the benediction. She hadn't missed the appraising looks of the other women in her small group.

She'd told them about him, of course, but clearly they thought she'd been exaggerating. Or making him up altogether.

Duncan leaned over to whisper in her ear. "Why are people staring?"

She glanced around. Two ladies who attended her Sunday school class were, in fact, staring. She smiled at them and lifted a hand. They quickly turned away. Anna shook her head. They'd been the two most vocally opposed to her going to Peacock Hill in May when she'd started asking for prayer as she made that decision. "No idea. They're from my group though, so maybe they're just wondering who you are."

The music changed and people started talking louder and reaching to gather their things.

"Do we need to go to your class?" Duncan picked up his Bible and hers. He smiled when she reached to take it from him. "I've got it."

He was so courteous. And kind. And just...perfect. Anna grinned. "No. It's all women. They'll understand."

"Should we at least go say hi?"

Anna shrugged. She hadn't planned to spend much time introducing Duncan to anyone, but that was simply because she didn't think anyone other than the ladies in her small group actually knew her name. So why would they care? "Sure."

The two women weren't sisters, but they'd been best friends since high school. They'd also made it very clear from Anna's first day that their friendship circles were quite full enough without her in them. Most of the ladies in the group had. They were fine with her coming to class, and the odd class-based social gathering. But she heard the whispers about unofficial gatherings and, after being rebuffed twice when asking about them, had realized she wasn't invited. Ever. She tried to squelch the lifting of her heart and the smile she feared bordered on smug as they approached.

"Morning, Anna. Who's this?"

"Hi Jane. Jill. I'd like you to meet Duncan McIntyre. I mentioned him a little in class? Duncan, these ladies are in my small group."

Duncan took each woman's hand and shook. "Lovely to meet you. I imagine you enjoy spending time with Anna as much as I do. I'm sorry to have taken up all her time this weekend."

Anna barely held back a laugh. The looks on Jane and Jill's faces were hilarious, though. Clearly, they weren't sure how to respond and were struggling to decide what to say that wouldn't reveal their true feelings.

"It's nice to meet you." Jane dimpled prettily when she smiled at Duncan before turning to Anna. "Will we see you in class?"

"Not today. Duncan has to head back to D.C. this afternoon." And it wasn't like he'd be welcome in an all-woman Bible study. Was she supposed to ditch him so she could still attend?

"Ah. Of course. We'll have to do lunch later this week."

Anna blinked and made a non-committal sound. Jill wanted to do lunch? Even three weeks ago that would've been tempting. But now? Now all Anna could do was wonder why.

"Come on, honey." Duncan kissed the top of Anna's head and slipped his fingers through hers. "Pleasure to meet both of you ladies."

Anna gave a half-wave as she turned away and started down the aisle to the foyer. She couldn't stop the laugh that bubbled out. "You realize that's the first time either of them have ever given me the time of day, right?"

"I gathered. I've seen enough of that with 'friends' of Deidre and Claire to know the type." Duncan shook his head. "Women are weird."

Anna grinned. "You won't get an argument from me. But there are exceptions. Like your sisters. And a few others. Most of us seem to outgrow high school by the time we're thirty."

"I'll take your word for it. Did you want to go to your class? I can find something else to do."

"No, it's fine. The rest of the girls aren't as bad as Jane and Jill, but they're still not what I'd call friends."

Duncan pulled open the door and held it as she walked out into the early summer sunshine. The humidity was already growing. Welcome to June in Virginia. She wrinkled her nose. Duncan slid on sunglasses. "Okay. Now what?"

"Lunch? And then maybe the botanical gardens before you have to leave?" The gardens were another favorite place to walk around and let her mind wander.

There were streams that wound through the different planting areas, a pond, and several sections with playground equipment for kids. Families often strolled through together and Anna had always enjoyed sitting and watching them, imagining what their lives must be like. With her hand in Duncan's...maybe today she'd be someone other people made up stories about.

"That sounds perfect." Duncan leaned over and kissed the tip of her nose.

Anna tilted her face until their lips met. The kiss was brief, but by no means perfunctory. And it left her feeling just a little off center in all the right ways.

16

"You're awfully chipper this week." Evan, Ken's lackey, draped his arm over the top of Duncan's cubicle. "Anything I should know about?"

Duncan saved the design he was working on and turned in his chair. "Just had a good weekend. Yourself?"

Evan seemed taken aback. "Oh. It was fine, I guess. But it's Wednesday."

"That it is. Did you need something?"

"Just wondered if you could cut down the humming. It's annoying."

He'd been humming? That wasn't like him at all. But Anna...she made his heart sing, it wasn't that surprising to hear the song was working its way out. "Sorry. I'll try to keep it down. If you need to borrow some headphones, I think I have an extra pair."

"No. Thanks." Evan knocked on the top of the cube before returning to his own space.

Duncan shook his head and pulled open a drawer. Maybe if he listened to music he wouldn't hum audibly. Humming. That was a new one. He plugged his headphones into the jack on his phone and tapped his favorite streaming service. A nice mix of 80s and 90s should do the trick.

He slipped the headphones on, leaving one ear partially uncovered so he'd be sure to hear the phone or anyone who came by needing something, and turned back to the design for a strip mall landscaping makeover. He'd designed for this management company earlier in the year and, according to the phone call he'd had on Monday, the increase in business stores were seeing was at least partially driven by his work. So they'd decided to give another faltering center a facelift and see if it helped.

Maybe it wasn't as fulfilling as helping homeowners maximize the potential of their lawns. But it had its rewards. And a satisfied client who came back was one of them. Not that he didn't get residential work. He did. But Marshall Brothers charged more than the average homeowner wanted to spend, so if a client wanted additional work, they often would ask if he could do it freelance. And as of yesterday, that was now specifically against company policy.

Duncan frowned. He was positive that change could be laid firmly at Ken's doorstep. He was also fairly certain that Evan was still doing freelance work. Because no matter how quiet you tried to be on the phone in a cube farm, your neighbors still overheard your conversations. But he wasn't going to be the one to go running to tattle. More than likely Evan had special dispensation, or would get it if Ken found out he needed it.

His phone rang. He slipped his headphones down around his neck and grabbed the handset. "Duncan McIntyre."

"Hi Duncan, it's your dad."

"Hey. What can I do for you?"

"Listening ears, I take it?"

"Usually."

His father sighed. "Okay, well I'll keep it short then. Do you think you could come by for dinner this week? Tonight, even? I wanted to talk to you about this garden idea your mother had before it got out of control."

"Yeah, I can make that work."

"Tonight?"

"Sure."

"Okay. Perfect. Come on by when you're done with work. And your mother wants to hear all about your weekend with Anna. So you're aware."

Duncan chuckled. "Of course. Thanks for calling."

"Oh sure. My pleasure. Goofy kid. Love you."

"You too. Bye." Duncan hung up the phone and scrubbed his hands over his face. He hated the idea that he had to hide helping his dad with a gardening project. But the memo had been explicit. No outside projects, including for family. It didn't seem like that was something the company could actually restrict though. If you were on your own time, wasn't that *your own time?* Except, who wanted to litigate it? Because that's what it'd turn into, if he tried to appeal the policy. He'd be better off quitting.

As he was about to put his headphones back on, the intercom on his phone buzzed. "McIntyre. My office."

Sure, Ken. No problem. Why waste time with niceties like "would you" and "please" or even a full sentence? Duncan sighed and set the headphones on his desk. What had he done now?

With a notebook and pen, he crossed through the cubes to knock on Ken's office door. "You wanted to see me?"

"Come in and shut the door." Ken barely looked up from his laptop.

Duncan did as instructed, standing by the exit. Maybe it'd be fast and he could get back to work. He should be able to finish the layout for the shopping center by lunch time. And then...then he might just work on his letter of resignation.

Ken finished typing and scooted his chair so he wasn't hidden behind the monitor. "Evan says you've been very loud the last two days."

Seriously? Evan complained to Ken about it? "He did stop by this morning to say something, sir. I've fixed the problem, I believe, but that was the first time it had been mentioned."

"Yes, well. It's important that we be respectful of the others who are busy working at their desks."

Did Ken *mean* to imply that Duncan wasn't working, or was that just a side benefit? What was there to say, though, really? "Yes, sir."

Ken pursed his lips and gave a curt nod. "Very well. As long as you understand. Now. Give me an update on the Bull Run Strip design."

The one that was sitting idle at his desk while he was in here talking to Ken? That design? Duncan seethed but forced a smile. "It's going very well. I should have a final design sent over before lunch."

"I'd like to have Evan review it before you send anything to the client."

Duncan began counting in his head. He got to twenty and was still ready to spit. "No, sir. I don't believe that's possible. The client contacted me, directly, as this is return business that I was directly and solely responsible for in the first place. I would need their permission before involving another associate."

"McIntyre, Evan *will* be approving your design before you send it. Are we clear?"

Duncan held Ken's gaze and refused to look away. Blood pounded in his head and his ears buzzed. "I believe I made myself clear. If you have nothing more, I'll return to work."

"Don't you walk out on me, McIntyre!" Ken's voice followed him into the hall between the cubicles. A few of his coworkers turned with raised eyebrows.

Duncan shook his head and stalked to his cube. He put on his headphones and, after a couple of calming breaths, unlocked his computer and returned to his design. He worked without interruption—well, ignoring the attempted interruptions—for another hour. The voice mail light on his phone flashed and he'd glimpsed three people leaving sticky notes on his white board when he'd refused to turn around. He went over the design once more before sending it off to his client.

He checked to ensure that the client's contact information was in his cell phone, along with the information of the handful of steady clients that he'd brought in to Marshall Brothers, before sorting through his desk drawers and removing anything personal from their contents. It all packed easily into the backpack he carried to work. He'd never taken the time to personalize his space here beyond a photo of his family and a couple of amusing cartoons. Then, before he could change his mind, he typed up a letter of resignation and printed it. He logged out of his computer, collected his bag, and aimed for the printer.

"McIntyre!"

Duncan shook his head as he walked past Ken's office, but not before he caught a glimpse of Evan relaxed in one of the guest chairs, smirking. Let him smirk. The joke was on them. Or it would be. He collected his printout and strode to the elevators, punching the call button that would let him go up to see Mr. Marshall in person. He fought the urge to glance over his shoulder. Would Ken and Evan chase him down? Or would they be content to wait until he, ostensibly, returned from lunch?

He checked the time on his phone. It was a little late for lunch, but still plausible. Especially since he'd already said he wanted to finish the design first.

Finally, the elevator arrived. Duncan stepped in and nodded to the woman inside. The right floor was already lit, so he pushed the "Door Close" button and had the satisfaction of seeing Evan peer out of Ken's office as the doors closed. The car rose slowly, finally stopping at the executive floor. He let the woman get off and took a deep breath. No going back. Not now.

He fixed a smile on his face and wound through the offices until he reached Mr. Marshall's administrative assistant. "Hi. I was hoping I could see Mr. Marshall? I don't have an appointment but..."

The woman frowned and consulted a book on her desk. "Let me check. Your name?"

"Duncan McIntyre." He glanced at her desk and pointed to the cup of pens. "May I borrow one of those?"

She nodded and picked up the phone.

Duncan took pen and looked at the resignation. This was the right thing. Maybe it's not how he'd have preferred to do it—but sometimes enough was enough. He scrawled his name at the bottom and replaced the pen in the cup.

"Mr. Marshall says to go right in."

"Thanks." Duncan stepped around her desk and knocked on the closed door before opening it a crack. "Mr. Marshall?"

"Duncan! It's good to see you. Come on in." Mr. Marshall grinned and rose from his seat behind a massive cherry desk. "Have a seat. Can I get you something to drink?"

"No, sir, thank you." Duncan eyed the chairs but didn't sit. "I won't take much of your time. I just wanted to give you this in person, in case you had any questions."

Mr. Marshall took the sheet of paper when Duncan offered it. Duncan looked around the office while the older gentleman read and then heaved a heavy sigh. "Won't you sit, please?"

Duncan cast a look over his shoulder before nodding and lowering himself into one of the leather visitor chairs.

"I can't say I wasn't expecting this, but it saddens me. There's nothing we can do to get you to stay?"

"Sir, respectfully, not if Ken is going to continue to try and micromanage things with the full support of Mr. Marshall, Junior. And...maybe it's not my place, but the memo from yesterday? About no jobs on our own time? I don't see how you can enforce that. And it's sown a lot of bad will amongst the designers."

"What's this?" Mr. Marshall frowned. "That's never been a policy of Marshall Brothers. The work people do for friends and family has always served as a reference for future clients."

Duncan shrugged. "You should talk to Ken, then. And Mr. Marshall, Junior, as his name was on the memo as well."

"Be sure I will." He cocked his head to the side. "But that's not why you're leaving us."

"No, sir." Duncan swallowed. He didn't want to burn bridges. Or look like a petulant child. And yet...Mr. Marshall deserved to know what was going on. So he related his interaction with Ken and the command that Evan review his work before he made contact with a client. And, since he was on a roll, he gave more details about past interactions and how Evan was being forced on everyone in varying ways, despite seemingly little ability of his own.

"You tried to tell me." The older man shook his head. "I'm afraid I discounted a lot of what you said. I'm sorry. I hate to see you leave us."

"Thank you, sir. That means a lot."

Now the man grinned. "But not enough to get you to stay. I understand a polite brush-off when I hear one. You keep my direct number, Duncan, and use it whenever you think I can help you. I mean that. You're a bright star, and I should've taken better care to keep you. You'll have a job here whenever you want it, as long as I'm around. What will you do?"

"I'm going to strike out on my own." The words made his heart race, but the still felt right. Solid. He smiled. "But don't worry—I'll be leaving the area, so I won't be in direct competition."

Mr. Marshall chuckled. "If anyone can do it, I believe you can. I wish you all the best. And I'm serious, if you need anything, ever, you give me a call."

Duncan stood and extended his hand. "Thank you, sir. I appreciate that. I've enjoyed my time here."

Mr. Marshall shook his hand with a firm grip. "If you think of it, drop me a line now and then and let me know how you're doing."

"Yes, sir."

"Oh, Duncan?"

Duncan turned.

Mr. Marshall tapped the resignation letter. "Did you give this to Ken?"

"No, sir. I brought it directly to you."

The man's grin resembled that of a shark. "Very good. Leave your badge with security in the garage. I'll let them know you're on the way down."

Duncan returned the grin and opened the office door. Maybe his leaving would make some changes for the people who were still here. The elevator doors opened as he approached, and he strode in and pushed the button for the garage. It was the end of one chapter, but the start of a new one full of exciting unknowns.

17

Anna hefted her duffel bag and pulled the apartment door shut behind her. This wasn't quite how she'd anticipated meeting Duncan's parents. Or his mom, at least, since she'd already met his dad. But a two-hour car trip while Duncan was in a moving truck behind them? Not exactly the plan.

"Hey. You're ready?" Duncan strode down the hall toward her and pulled her into a tight hug.

"Why can't I ride with you in the truck again?" Anna's hands tightened into fists on the straps of her bag. "I'm not sure..."

"There isn't room to move the boxes in the passenger seat of the truck into Mom and Dad's car—I tried. You're going to be fine, I promise. You've met Dad, and Mom's dying to meet you. Please?"

She sighed. How was she supposed to resist that look? "Okay."

He grinned and kissed her.

She leaned into it, prolonging the contact. Maybe it was more than he intended, but she needed the reminder of why she was doing this.

"I love you." He eased back and tapped her nose. "Come on, they're waiting."

"They really don't mind dropping me off on Sunday?"

"Not at all."

Anna forced a smile. Two hours in the car together. Plus the weekend with them at Peacock Hill. And then two hours for the drive back to Richmond. Why had she agreed again? Oh, that's right. Duncan had quit his job and was moving down there. She'd wanted to be with him—even though she wouldn't be able to join him until July. She'd put her notice in, but they were insisting on the full two weeks. Which was reasonable. They weren't at all happy she was leaving and had tried to push for a month's notice. But she'd held firm and finally they'd agreed. It gave her time to get everything in order. How Duncan had managed as quickly as he did was a mystery. Although...not really. He'd been supremely organized in college, too. And that was not her defining characteristic.

They left the building and she laughed at the moving truck, complete with a trailer hauling Duncan's car, parked beside a sedan in the visitor parking. "How did you get the truck in that space?"

"It wasn't terrible. Just a little wiggle this way, then that. Out should be easier." He tapped on the driver side window of his parents' car.

The window rolled down and Wade grinned. "Hi Anna. It's so nice to meet you again."

She smiled and lifted a hand in greeting. "Hello, Mr. McIntyre. Mrs. McIntyre."

"Wade, please. I'm serious. And this is Katie."

Katie leaned across Wade and grinned. "Hi, honey. I feel like I know you already. You set?"

Anna swallowed and cast a pleading look at Duncan. He either didn't see it or he ignored it as he pulled open the rear door and kissed her cheek. "I guess so."

"You'll be fine." Duncan patted her shoulder as she slid into the backseat and pushed her duffel to the floor. He turned to look at his dad. "Want me to lead?"

"Since you know where you're going, that seems like a good plan." Wade chuckled. "Get going. We promise not to eat her alive."

Duncan laughed and patted the top of the car. "See ya at the Hill."

"Right." Anna reached for her seatbelt and clicked it into place.

Katie shifted in her seat and beamed at Anna. "Now, tell me everything about yourself."

Her stomach dropped. This was worse than a job interview. She was going to kill Duncan.

Deidre was standing on the front steps, bouncing up and down as the car came to a stop in front of

Peacock Hill. Duncan's truck was already parked by the front stairs, but he wasn't in the cab. Anna unhooked her seatbelt and pushed open the door, taking in a deep breath of the clean mountain air. She'd missed that in Richmond.

Deidre grabbed her in a tight hug. "I'm so glad you could come, too!"

"What, no hug for your old man?" Wade stepped out of the car with a grin and held his arms open.

"Oh, I guess." Deidre laughed and hugged her dad. "I'm so glad you two finally made it down."

"Finally? You've only been here since March." Katie stepped out of the car and stretched her back and arms. "Gosh, I don't miss road trips."

Deidre chuckled and rounded the car to hug her mom and kiss her cheek. "I appreciate you doing it for me."

Arm in arm, mother and daughter turned to face the mansion. Katie nodded. "It's even more beautiful in person, sweetheart. God's going to do some amazing things with this place."

"You think so, Mom?" Deidre rested her head on her mom's shoulder. "That's my hope."

"If that's what you're setting out to do, then I have faith God will bless it." Katie kissed Deidre's head.

Anna blinked back tears. Katie made her homesick for her mom. And it was so obvious Katie loved Duncan and wanted the best for him. When Anna's parents had lived in Richmond, they'd been close like that. Anna would stop by after work, or she and her mom would go out on Saturday for girl time. When they'd left, they'd taken away one of the solid pillars Anna had built her life on. Duncan was lucky to have Katie and Wade. Did he know it?

"Hey, you okay?" Duncan appeared at her side and slid his arm around her waist.

She cleared her throat. "Of course. I like your folks."

He grinned. "I hoped you would."

Wade broke away from where he stood with Katie and Deidre and clapped his hands together. "Let's see these gardens I've heard so much about."

Anna's gaze darted to Deidre. "Don't you want to see inside first?"

"No. Let's save that for when Claire's back. She should be here any minute. Since she's been helping a lot lately, the inside is as much hers as mine." Deidre tucked her hands in her pockets.

Wade's eyebrows rose. "You got your sister to drive somewhere? By herself?"

Deidre grinned. "Around here she has little choice. She's adapting."

"Well, keep her away from my car." Duncan laughed. "I'm still not sure I trust her."

Anna shook her head and pointed to the side of the house. "Let's head this way and start with one of the sunken gardens Duncan restored."

Duncan caught her hand in his and they stepped out together. Anna glanced behind her to make sure everyone was following. It was good to be back here.

With Duncan. It was right. She wasn't ever going to want to leave.

Anna looked around the long table that filled Peacock Hill's dining room. It had to be at least eighteen feet. Where on earth had Deidre found such a thing? She ran her hand over the glossy wood. It was almost too pretty to eat at. And for all that it was enormous, it didn't overwhelm the space.

Deidre clomped into the room, her arms full of dishes. "Like it?"

"It's gorgeous. Like it was made for the room."

"Turns out, it was." Deidre grinned. "Jeremiah and his dad do woodworking. Who knew, right? They brought it up this afternoon while you and Duncan were out at Lover's Lake."

Anna's cheeks got hot. "You are *not* calling it that."

Deidre's eyes sparkled. "Why not? Jeremiah and I have been known to walk around back there, too, when we wanted a little more privacy than you can find in the gardens just yet."

"Just...no. I'll help you come up with a better name."

"Spoilsport." Deidre stuck out her tongue. "Want to help set the table?"

"Sure." Anna reached for a stack of plates. "What are we using for chairs?"

"Sadly, the folding chairs against the wall. They've assured me they're making chairs to match, but those take longer."

Anna nodded. That made sense. Chairs had more parts. "How many?"

"For tonight?"

"No, chairs."

"Twenty." Deidre nodded. "I know. But the table can handle it and with smaller retreats or weddings, it makes catering a more interesting prospect. And there's room for more round tables in the other rooms. It'd be spread out but...there are possibilities."

Anna grunted. It made sense. And the table was lovely. "So you're not planning on furniture in the other rooms down here on the main floor? Something suited to the original purpose?"

"See? I'm torn. The music room, in particular. But, barring that one, whatever I put in can probably be moved out of the way, or...I don't know. Maybe I need to talk to the types of people who might be using the space and figure out what they'd like to see before I worry about furnishings." Deidre set down her last plate and moved back to the end of the table to collect a handful of forks and napkins.

"I...might know someone. When we get to that point, I'll see if he can come out and do a consult." Anna smiled, thinking of her neighbor—soon to be ex-neighbor—and his flourishing event-planning business. If

Claire hadn't clearly already set her sights on Danny, Anna might suggest that she and Sean would hit it off. Still, he could make suggestions. He ran all kinds of events. And who knew? Maybe he'd want to bring some of his groups out this way.

"Cool." Deidre flashed a brilliant smile her way. "Maybe he could come sooner than later? I'm at the point where I need to decide what to do in the basement."

"Already?"

Deidre nodded. "We've got the second floor basically ready and we've made good progress on the third. If we keep going like this, we might be ready to start booking in early fall. Claire's trying to nail down that timeline."

That was impressive. But then, Deidre was a powerhouse in a tiny package. And she worked hard. Anna set the last place setting. "When are people going to get here?"

"Should be soon. In fact, if you don't mind manning the door, I should go check on the food." Deidre bustled back to the kitchen without waiting for Anna to agree. She shrugged. Minding the door was easy enough. And then she'd be the first to know when Duncan got back from wherever he'd gone with his parents.

Anna chuckled as Wade finished a story about Duncan as a small child. "That's so cute."

"Yeah...it's awesome. Dad." Duncan sent his father a pointed glare.

Wade held up his hands. "That was the last one, promise."

"Well, I make no such promise." Katie laughed and pushed her empty plate toward the middle of the table. "You were an adorable little boy and gave us lots of good laughs."

From the stories they'd told this evening, Anna had to agree. She leaned closer to Duncan so her voice wouldn't carry. "Don't worry, I still love you."

He turned his head and held her gaze, a smile at the corners of his lips. "That's good to hear. When do I get to meet your parents?"

"Next time they visit from California. Unless you want to take a trip out there?"

Duncan frowned. "That hardly seems fair. You know all my childhood secrets—"

"Not all of them. There are plenty more where those came from." Claire waggled her eyebrows as she leaned around Duncan to intrude on the conversation. "So if you want more, just come find me. Ow."

Danny managed to look innocent from his seat across from Claire. "Sorry. My leg slipped."

Claire rolled her eyes and tapped her chest mouthing the words, "Come to me."

Anna grinned. Since she was sharing a room with Claire, she'd have to hit her up for more stories later tonight. She turned her head at the sound of a fork dinging against a glass.

"If I could get your attention?" Jeremiah set down his glass and stood.

"What are you doing?" Deidre tugged on his arm.

Jeremiah smiled at her and leaned down to kiss her forehead. "I wanted to propose a toast. Even though we all have iced tea, it's good Southern sweet tea and well-suited to toasting in my mind."

"Hear, hear!" Danny grinned and raised his glass in a salute.

Jeremiah cleared his throat. "And I thought it was especially fitting to do now, when my parents and Mr. and Mrs. McIntyre are present."

"Wade." Mr. McIntyre shot Jeremiah a stern look.

"And Katie." Mrs. McIntyre followed suit.

Jeremiah's cheeks colored. "Pardon me, Mom and Dad and Wade and Katie are in attendance."

Wade clapped his hands and shot Deidre a wink.

Jeremiah tucked one hand in his pocket and used the other to lift his glass. "To Deidre McIntyre, an amazing woman who's doing an amazing job bringing Peacock Hill back to her former glory, the woman I love, and who I hope will agree to become my wife."

Anna chuckled as Deidre's cheeks went from pink to pale in an instant.

"Wait. What?" Deidre looked around before her gaze latched on Jeremiah.

He pulled a ring out of his pocket and sank to his knee. "Will you marry me?"

Deidre paused before grinning and reaching for Jeremiah. "Of course I will."

Anna clapped her hands and soon the whole table was applauding the embracing couple. "That's lovely."

Duncan wiped his cheek.

"Aww. You're tearing up." Anna patted his arm.

"It's not every day your little sister gets engaged." Duncan slipped his arm around the back of Anna's chair and pulled her closer. "It's not every day you get to be there when she does."

"I'm not normally a fan of the public proposal, but this was nice." Anna snuggled against Duncan's side and laid her head on his shoulder.

"I'll keep that in mind."

Anna blinked. He would? Was he...no. There was no way he was thinking about marriage. Was he? The conversation she'd had with Deidre came back to mind. Maybe she'd been fishing even then? She loved him, there was no question. And she wanted to spend her life with him. But she wasn't in a hurry to start. Was that wrong?

18

One week down, and another to go before Anna would be here on a more permanent basis. And then...Duncan sighed. Then what? They'd been talking on the phone every night, but it wasn't the same as being together every day. Working together. Would they be able to do this long-term?

Duncan printed the design he'd worked up for Mr. and Mrs. Crawford. Jeremiah, at least, had been true to his word and was referring the bulk of his landscaping work instead of taking it on. Even from his parents. The man knew his limitations. And it seemed like he was keeping busy enough with his lawn mowing and handyman jobs. Which was good. Duncan didn't want to take work that Jeremiah needed.

"Hey, you heading over to the Crawfords' soon?" Deidre pulled a chair out from the table she'd set up in the front room. They all used it, off and on, as their desk. There was a printer set up in the corner. Best of all, it was away from the bulk of the construction noise that was happening on the third floor.

"Yeah. Just finished the design. Why?"

"Can I come along? Claire's tiling the new bathroom on the third and is grouchy. She thinks I'm micromanaging."

"Are you?"

Deidre frowned. "No. But I can't start on my next project until she's done in there."

Duncan shrugged. "Fine with me if you tag along, but I don't know if Jeremiah's going to be there."

Deidre looked down at her left hand and smiled. "That's okay. I just need to get out of the house, you know?"

He did know. Restlessness was a major factor into his decision to do landscaping in the first place. He didn't mind sitting at a desk to put designs together, but that was primarily because he got to spend more time on site once the preliminary work was done. The personal touch—being at the job and supervising the contractors—had earned him the respect of many of his clients at Marshall Brothers. Now, keeping up with that practice would serve him well since he'd be doing a lot of the install until they built up enough business to afford hiring it out. If they even wanted to go that route. He made a mental note to talk to Anna about it.

"All right. Let's go. Grab my printouts, would you?" Duncan stood and flipped the lid of his laptop closed.

Deidre crossed to the printer and grabbed the papers, flipping through them. "These are nice. They're really letting you redesign the front?"

"That's what they said. I guess we'll see." He jangled the keys in his pockets. This was his first major proposal for the new company. It mattered. Which probably accounted for the churning his stomach was doing. The Crawfords were nice people. He'd just keep reminding himself that the whole way there.

Duncan unlocked his car as they went down the steps.

"You can leave it unlocked out here, you know?" Deidre jogged to keep up with him.

He slowed his pace. "Old habits and all that. I'll work on it. You think they'll like the designs?"

"I can't see why they wouldn't. It's a big improvement. And great advertising for you. Their neighborhood is full of folks who seem to get a great amount of joy in competing for best on the block. What'd Anna think?" Deidre slid into the passenger seat.

"Anna? She hasn't seen them." Duncan started the car and backed carefully around Deidre's truck before heading down the long driveway to the road into town.

"Why not?"

"What do you mean?"

"She's your business partner, right?"

"Yeah. So?"

Deidre sighed. "So, don't you think she ought to have a say in the designs you propose to new clients?"

Should she? He frowned. He had no intention of looking over her work. Why would she want to look over his? "I don't need someone looking over my shoulder. I know what I'm doing."

"I'm not questioning that, Duncan." Deidre drew in a breath as he pulled out onto the road just as another car came around the corner. "But...are you sure there isn't an expectation that you both agree with every client plan? After all, it's both of your reputations here. Not just yours."

They hadn't discussed that aspect of things at all. He'd assumed—and okay, he knew how to spell assume—that she agreed with him about not needing someone looking over her shoulder. If she wanted help and asked for it, that was one thing. Or an opinion. Didn't have to be help. But if not? This wasn't college anymore.

Duncan stretched out on his bed and looked around the room he'd claimed on the third floor. For now, at least, it was almost as cozy as his apartment had been. A lot of his things were stored—along with Deidre and Claire's stuff—in one of the basement rooms. There simply wasn't a need for three full kitchens worth of pots and pans. At least Claire had still been living at home, so she didn't have living room furniture down there, too.

He frowned. He could probably use his chairs and coffee table in this room. The couch wouldn't fit, but there was room enough for a little sitting area. He had his desk set up in the corner by the windows that looked out over the sunken garden. It was nice to be able to look out and, with minimal movement, see a fountain burbling away below. The bed was shoved in the opposite corner. He didn't need to be able to get around both sides. And if he only had one option for getting in and out, it meant he could never get up on the wrong one. Or so ran the theory. Regardless, there was room for at least the chairs. Duncan swung his legs over the side of the bed. He'd head down to the basement and haul them up.

His cell rang with the special ringtone he'd assigned to Anna. He smiled and lay back down. He'd get the chairs later.

"Hey you."

"Hey yourself." She had a smile in her voice and he could picture her in the living room of her apartment. "How was your day?"

He shifted so he could look out the window to the Blue Ridge Mountains on the horizon. "Really good. I took the plans over to the Crawfords. They're excited and ready to go. It's nice to have enthusiastic clients. As I was getting ready to go, their next-door neighbor came out. Turns out, he heard the Crawfords were putting in a fountain, and now he's thinking of a water feature in his back yard now, too."

Anna laughed. "They really do try to outdo one another, don't they?"

"Seems like. Good business for us, though, as he's asked me to put something together."

"Nice. I can't wait to get down there so I can help."

Duncan rubbed his chin. Help. That meant get her own clients, right? He cleared his throat. "About that. How are you envisioning this working, once you're here?"

"What do you mean?"

He sat up and moved to his desk chair. "Well, the business plan didn't go into a ton of specifics, so I sort of figured it'd be a lot like how it was, is, at Marshall Brothers."

"Which is...?"

Duncan winced. Now she sounded wary. And hurt? He had two sisters. He wasn't completely inept when it came to deciphering their tone. "Well, you know, every associate had their own clients and handled them. I mean, you could get help or opinions from people if you need them, but otherwise you just did the work. Right?"

There was a long pause before she spoke. "Sure. Of course."

He closed his eyes and pinched the bridge of his nose. Three words that meant exactly the opposite of what they sounded like when they came from an annoyed woman. "How were you thinking it would go?"

"Doesn't matter. That's fine." Her voice was clipped. He half-expected her to mention the time and hang up.

"It...doesn't sound fine." Why? Why was he going there? He should just take her words at face value and run with it. Except. He sighed. Except he loved her and he wanted their relationship *and* their business partnership to work. He sent up a quick prayer for help.

"No. It is. It's not what I imagined. But there's nothing wrong with it. I guess I thought we'd be working together on stuff. Collaborating, you know?"

"We'll probably have to work together on the installs. At least until we can afford to hire contractors to do some of it. But the design work? You wanted to collaborate on that, too?" Hadn't she hated him—or at least acted like she did—in college because he criticized her design ideas? Why would he volunteer for that on any sort of regular basis?

He'd let her take ownership of her projects at Peacock Hill because he had faith in her ability. If they'd been working together, there were tweaks he would've suggested. Not big ones. And in the grand scheme of things, neither better nor worse than what she put together. He hadn't because he didn't want to go down that road with her again. He wanted to be on a road where love—marriage, eventually—was a possibility.

"I figured we would, yeah." She sighed. "It's fine. I'll just have to adjust how I was thinking is all."

"Why don't you pray about it? I will too. Maybe I'm the one who needs to change the way I think." *Please Lord, don't let that be the case. I want to work with her, not fight with her constantly.*

"Okay."

He nodded. Time for a subject change. "How was your second-to-last Friday at the archives?"

19

Anna grabbed her Bible and stood. She wasn't going to small group today. They were going to ask about her upcoming move and all those details and...she wasn't convinced anymore that moving was the right thing to do. She wanted her mom and dad. Talking to them on the phone wasn't the same. Besides which, they were still annoyed that she'd been willing to quit at the archives and move to start her own business with Duncan when they'd suggested the same thing three years ago when they were moving to California to be near her brother and his family.

But she didn't want to live in California and design succulent gardens with rocks. And maybe that was unfair. There were probably some lovely landscaping options for some areas of the state. But when all that was on the news was the constant water shortage, it didn't give a lot of confidence about her ability to start up a business that relied on people's willingness to spend money for something that needed to be watered.

She squeezed past a clump of people in the aisle, muttering an apology under her breath.

"Hey, Anna. Wait." One of the guys in the clump turned and caught her arm.

"Wha—oh. Hi, Sean."

He frowned, turned back to the group to say something she didn't catch, and slapped a high five before falling into step with her. "You don't look happy. What's up?"

"Nothing."

"Seriously? We dated for four months and have been neighbors for years. I know when you're not happy. I saw it a lot."

Her lips twitched. "It wasn't that bad."

Sean clutched his chest and made a gasping sound.

Anna slapped his arm, laughing. "You're such a weirdo."

"I prefer the term 'loveable goofball'."

"You would." She smiled. The one thing Sean had always been able to do was make her laugh. When he'd asked her out, it had seemed like the recipe for a successful, long-term relationship. Boy, had she been wrong. Maybe she was wrong about Duncan, too.

"So. Are you going to tell me what's up or am I going to have to lay on the charm?" Sean pulled open the door to the parking lot. "I have a lot of that, too, if you recall."

Anna frowned and put a finger to her lips, pretending to think. "No. No, I don't quite recall that."

"Man. You're brutal today." Sean poked her shoulder. "Must be bad. Come on, I'm taking you to lunch and you're telling me all your woes."

"Sean, I appreciate..." Anna sighed. What was she going to do? Go home and sulk? "You know what, fine. Maybe you can give me some insight into the workings of the male mind."

"Oh ho. Trouble in paradise?" Sean took her arm and steered her toward his car. "I heard a rumor you two were going into business together and practically engaged."

"Business, yes. Neither of us has mentioned marriage. We've only been dating two months." And that was a bit of a stretch, depending on how you looked at it.

"Ah, but you're old flames, right? Or did my source get that part of the story wrong, too?" Sean started the car and joined the line of traffic leaving the church parking lot.

Old flames? Who had he been talking to, her mom? Mom had loved him...and Anna wouldn't put it past Mom to keep up with him in hopes of pushing them together again in the future. "We knew each other in college. Did some projects together, that kind of thing. Old flames is a bit of a stretch."

"That's not how I heard it. I heard there were mutual crushes and twin flames of unrequited passion simmering under the surface."

Anna snickered. "You started watching soap operas again, didn't you?"

Sean shrugged. "You work from home and tell me if you don't need the company sometime. I got tired of watching people who can't make up their mind about paint colors and whether or not they were going to learn to love the house they already bought or spend money they didn't have to move to a house they'd probably hate in five years anyway."

"Simmering passion is better?"

"Yes. Simmering passion is always better. I think we could all do with some simmering passion—handled in a pure and God-honoring manner, of course—in our lives. Don't you?"

Anna sighed. Whether or not they'd had it in college—and okay, sure, she'd had the unrequited interest thing going on—they definitely had it now. "I'm not sure. It just seems to complicate things."

"Hmmm." Sean pulled into the parking lot of a strip mall and maneuvered through the rows of cars until he found a spot. "Come on. You need corned beef and sauerkraut."

A Reuben did sound good. But then, when didn't it? Had he...he had. Her favorite hole-in-the-wall deli. Which he hated. "We don't have to go here."

"I think we do. You need cheering up. Besides, I found I can tolerate their French dip. Even if sandwiches, as a breed, are bizarre and unwieldy things." Sean bumped her shoulder. "So, since we know that even good looks and charm can't make you fall in love with someone who doesn't enjoy eating with their hands, tell me about Duncan, why you love him, and what's making you sad."

Anna laughed. "It wasn't your sandwich phobia. You know that, right?"

"Shh. Don't say that. Then I'd have to spend time in self-examination and figure out what I keep doing wrong."

"All right, you're right, we wouldn't want that." She shook her head. They'd both agreed there was no chemistry. He knew that. "You're a great guy, Sean. You just need to find the woman God has for you."

"It's like you're breaking up with me all over again." He winked. "Good thing my heart's not invested this time or I might make you buy your own sandwich."

"I'm serious."

"So am I. I don't buy sandwiches for every girl I'm friends with." He shooed her toward an empty table. "Go and sit. I know what you want."

It was good someone did. Anna looked at her friend for a moment before weaving through the tightly packed seating area toward an empty spot in the back corner.

He was back before long with a metal stand holding the number nine and two soft drinks. Sean pushed one cup toward her before taking a seat and setting their order number in the middle of the table. "Try it. It's new."

Anna winced. New and soda weren't things that went together all that well in her experience. She took a small sip. "Cherry cola isn't new."

"Gotcha." Sean grinned and sipped his own drink. "Now, spill it."

Anna took another drink and launched into the story of her work in the archives for Deidre and how it led to her going out to Peacock Hill, the reunion with Duncan, the undeniable chemistry between them, his misery at work, her own misery at the archives, and the new business. In the middle of the story, a waitress dumped their plates on the table and whisked away the metal stand. She'd paused for Sean to say a blessing over their food, and then continued. Since Sean had a good head on his shoulders and, for all his goofing around, had never been as serious about the two of them as he pretended, she spared no details.

"Which brings us to now. And I'm seriously wondering if I've misread the whole situation and need to figure out if the archives will let me un-resign." Her stomach twisted. She didn't want to keep working there. But the reality was, she hadn't found a sublet for her apartment, so if she did move, she'd either have to break the lease—which would cost money she didn't have—or keep paying the rent each month even though she no longer lived there. And that seemed stupid.

Sean dipped a French fry into the jus that came with his sandwich. "Let me see if I understand. He quit his job at major prestigious D.C. firm because his boss was making a power play and trying to have someone look over his designs—presumably to alter or critique them in some way—before he sent them to the client. And now you're upset because it wasn't his thought process that the two of you would look over each other's designs—presumably to alter or critique them in some way—before he took them to your private clients?"

Anna hunched her shoulders. "When you put it that way…"

"What way would you put it?"

"We're a team, right? Partners? Don't partners work together? Share things?" She waved her dill pickle spear as she spoke before chomping off one end.

"Sure. But that's different than double-checking his work."

"I never said anything about double-checking. Just working together."

"Ok, that's fair. What does working together mean to you?" Sean dunked another fry.

Anna wrinkled her nose. "You know God made ketchup for fries, right? Not…greasy meat juice."

"Thus says the woman currently eating corned beef slathered in salad dressing and topped with cabbage. I won't critique your taste buds, if you'll leave mine alone, too. Deal?"

She stuck out her tongue and shuddered as he dipped more fries into the jus and made exaggerated yummy sounds as he put them in his mouth. "Fine."

"So. Team work?"

Anna took a bite of the Reuben, licked the dressing that oozed out from between the bread off her thumb, and chewed. What did team work mean? She swallowed and sipped her cola. "I guess I thought we'd design together. I figured if we were working at the same computer, talking through each step, there wouldn't be an opportunity for him to disregard my opinions, you know?"

"He does that a lot?"

She shook her head. "Not anymore. But in college—"

"Ten years ago, when he was considerably less mature, as most college-age guys are."

"Right." She took another bite. "You're saying I'm overreacting."

"Not necessarily. I mean, you feel how you feel. So you're upset that he doesn't want to work with you because...?"

Why did it bother her? She didn't want him overriding her opinions and choices. At first glance, each of them handling their own clients should sound ideal. But the reality was, he had a lot more experience than she did. And good instincts. "I guess I don't know if I'm good enough to be on my own. Maybe he's already figured that out and doesn't want his name tied to mine."

Sean started to laugh, his humor trailing off when she ducked her head. "Oh. You're serious."

She nodded.

"Anna, look at me."

She sighed and lifted her gaze to meet Sean's.

"Nobody starts a business with someone if they don't think their work is up to whatever standards they have. If you hadn't been confident in Duncan's ability, would partnering up ever have crossed your mind?"

She shook her head.

"Right. Add in the fact that he loves you and, from what I've gathered, you love him? He wants his name tied to yours in even more permanent ways than at the bottom of a landscape layout."

Who was his source? "You're still talking to my mom, aren't you?"

Sean grinned. "That's for me to know and you to guess. But even if I am, which I'm neither confirming nor denying, the logic holds."

"Barring one major problem. I don't have the experience he does, so he's justified in wondering if I can handle the work and do a good job. *I* wonder if I can do it. Sure, it's my degree, but that piece of paper is ten years old and has never really been put to the test."

"Please. Who designed the prayer garden at the church?"

"I did. But that was easy. Anyone could've—"

"Zzt. What about all the pop up mission projects the youth did for the elderly and disadvantaged around town last summer? I seem to recall anything that had to do with yards was run by you beforehand. Correct?"

"Just for form. Again, we're talking something anyone who watches TV could do."

He glared. "A little humility is a good thing. I'll be the first to say that. But you've taken it too far and crossed the line into sin. You're downplaying a God-given gift that you use beautifully for Him whenever you get the chance. Now you have the opportunity to use it full-time for profit. That's great. I don't understand why you're running away."

Anna bristled. She wasn't running away. She was just...exercising a little overdue caution. Which was not sinful. "I'm not scared."

"Didn't say you were." He dunked his sandwich and took a big bite. "Didn't say you weren't either."

"So helpful." Anna poked at her food. "Let's change the subject."

"Hey. I just want to see you happy. And it seems to me that Duncan is part of that."

"Thanks. Really." It was too bad they were better off as friends. Sean was a great guy. And he'd make someone an excellent husband. Hopefully whoever it was would let him still be Anna's friend. "Tell me something crazy from your latest big event."

20

Duncan pushed his flatbed cart down the rows of shrubs at the Charlottesville garden center and focused on not stewing. He was here to shop, that's it. He and Anna hadn't stayed together for long when they were there, so there shouldn't be too many memories of her following him around.

She hadn't called since Friday.

She didn't pick up when he called her.

Which was fine. She was busy. Or out. Though it wasn't like he was calling a landline, so 'out' didn't really fly. Whatever. Busy. That still worked. And mulling it over wasn't going get the plants that he needed for the Crawfords' front yard picked out and into Deidre's truck. With doing smaller residential jobs like this, he needed to consider buying a truck of his own. Or their own. For the business. It was just one other thing he'd wanted to talk to Anna about.

"Duncan?"

He turned and smiled. "Hey, Tom. This isn't your usual area, is it?"

"I've been known to dabble in plant life as well as water features. They encourage all employees to be

knowledgeable around here. What brings you back?"
Tom hooked his thumbs in his front pockets. "You get
that lion fountain running?"

"I did. Everything at Peacock Hill is looking
good. I'm actually working on a residential job today."

"With Marshall Brothers? They don't usually take
residential this far down, do they? We've had some
inquiries lately and are trying to figure out where to refer
them."

"I'm not with MB anymore. I decided to take my
sister up on her offer to manage the grounds and set out
a shingle."

"You're taking jobs?"

"Yeah. Did you meet Anna Hamilton when she
was here? Same day I was?"

Tom nodded. "Briefly. I think."

"She's my business partner. So between the two
of us, we've got room for a decent client load."

"Nice. You going to be around a few?"

Duncan looked at his practically empty cart and
laughed. "At least."

"Great. Don't disappear without finding me, if I
don't find you first."

"Okay. Thanks." He pushed the cart a little bit
down the aisle and stopped in front of the euonymous.
They had the gold splash and the white album and the
mixture of the two shades of variegated leaves would add
the depth and difference he was looking for. He hauled
two of each onto his cart and consulted the list on his
phone. Maybe he ought to have considered delivery.

Even with reusing as much as he could safely transplant, he was going to need at least one more flatbed.

Duncan had parked the first cart by the register and had a second one nearly full when Tom finally came jogging toward him.

"Sorry about that. Seemed like every time I turned around, I got stopped."

Duncan grinned. "I know how that goes."

"Okay, so here are the contact numbers for the five people who've called us in the last...week and half, ish? They're looking for what sounds like pretty straightforward residential work, but we just don't have the people to handle it, and the owner really isn't interested in expanding that direction."

Duncan frowned. That seemed short-sighted. "Why not?"

Tom shrugged. "I'm not sure. They used to have people on staff for just this kind of thing, but something obviously soured them on it. Anyway, Mrs. Landsdowne wanted to make sure you were okay with them giving out your name and number to anyone who called."

"Yeah? Yeah. Of course. Anna should be full-time at the end of the week, so she can jump right in. I...wow. Thanks. This is great."

"Don't mention it. I've seen the kind of work you do, so the referral's easy as far as I'm concerned. And if you need to buy stock, well..."

Duncan chuckled. "Be sure I'll go through you guys. No worries there."

"Mrs. L. only cares about the jobs you get through us, but it's not like we're going to turn you away."

"Hope not. I don't want to have to deal with the big box stores. Their plants always seem so sad."

"That's because they are." Tom grinned and extended his hand.

Duncan shook it, mirroring the man's expression. "I'm glad I ran into you. You should come by and see the fountains at Peacock Hill sometime."

"I'll try to do that. Any idea when the house is going to be open? The wife's desperate for a look inside."

"Nothing firm yet, but I'll keep you posted. Hey, Tom, you wouldn't happen to know a florist, would you?"

"What kind are you looking for?"

"Deidre—my sister—is turning Peacock Hill into a retreat center and wedding venue. Weddings equals flowers, right? She's no business slouch, so she'd like to have someone who she can either recommend or require, depending."

Tom drummed his fingers on his leg. "I might have just the person for you, but I need to check a few things."

"No rush. We're not open yet. But anyone you can send our way would be great."

"Would they have to work exclusively with you?"

Duncan shook his head. "Don't think so, unless she gets so busy that they wouldn't have time for outside jobs."

"Okay. I'll need your number—both for referrals from here and then in case the person I have in mind is interested."

Duncan dug in his pocket for two business cards. "Got a pen?"

Tom took the pencil from behind his ear and offered it.

"That works." Duncan x'd out the front of the cards and flipped it over, printing his name and cell number on the back of both cards before handing them to Tom. "Thanks, man."

"You got it." He looked at the nearly full flatbed. "You need a hand?"

"I wouldn't turn one down when it comes time to load everything in the truck. I have a little more I need to get."

Tom nodded. "Have them page me when they start ringing you up."

"Will do. Thanks again." Duncan loaded a few more pots onto the cart before pushing it toward the front of the garden center. Anna was going to flip. His stomach knotted. If she actually picked up. He sighed and it seemed like the sun dimmed a little. What was going on with her? With them?

Duncan parked the empty truck under one of the cedars near the front of Peacock Hill and dragged himself up the steps. That was a lot of hauling for one day. And tomorrow would be more of it, and digging. But the end result would be worth it. Seeing Mrs. Crawford's face light up as she looked over the plants he'd bought had made that clear.

He pulled open the front door and aimed for the stairs and the siren call of a hot shower.

"Hey, you're back." Deidre peeked out of the kitchen door and smiled. "Come have a snack and tell me how it went."

Duncan glanced wistfully at the stairs. He'd been so close. "Can it wait?"

"Um. Not really? But it won't take long, I promise."

Sighing, Duncan took his foot off the first step and followed his sister into the kitchen. Claire and Jeremiah were at the kitchen table with glasses in front of them. There was a plate of cookies in between them.

"What can I get you to drink?" Deidre stood by the fridge.

"Any coffee?" Duncan sat next to Claire and snagged a cookie from the plate.

"I can make a pot."

He shook his head. "Never mind. Just...what's that? Lemonade?"

"Yeah. Claire made it." Deidre opened the fridge and pulled out a pitcher.

"Even better."

"Hey. My lemonade isn't bad. Tell him, Jeremiah." Deidre sent her fiancé a pointed look.

"Oh. Right. She's right." Jeremiah waited until Deidre turned her back before shaking his head and mouthing the words, "Claire's is better."

Duncan chuckled.

"I heard that." Deidre set a glass in front of Duncan and punched Jeremiah's shoulder as she sat down next to him. She pointed a finger at her sister. "You'd better stop showing me up, missy."

"Maybe you should step up your game a little?" Claire grinned and bit into a cookie. "Although these are tasty. You made these, right?"

"No. Those would be from my mother." Jeremiah reached for the plate. "In appreciation for everything Duncan is doing at their house. She texted me after you left. The plants you chose made a big impression."

"Good one, right?" Duncan took a sip of the lemonade and shivered as the tart liquid hit his tongue.

"Definitely. I knew you'd do better than I would." Jeremiah grinned. "So, thanks. I heard Mr. Cliffton is after you to do his now, too?"

"Yeah. Have they always been like that?" Duncan glanced over his shoulder at the door. There was a hot shower out there calling his name. And as much as he loved his sisters and enjoyed Jeremiah...it wasn't clear why this couldn't have waited.

"Pretty much. Though Mom and Mrs. Cliffton were best buds before she passed, so it was always good-natured. I think it just helps Mr. Cliffton keep his wife alive." Jeremiah shrugged.

Claire cleared her throat. "Since I've now seen you looking at the door twice, maybe we should cut to the chase?"

"I'd like that. No offense. I'm just really tired." Duncan reached for another cookie.

"Right. Okay, so Anna texted me this afternoon and said she wasn't going to be coming down this weekend as originally planned." Deidre leaned forward and held Duncan's gaze. "Did you know?"

Reeling, Duncan shook his head. He set down the cookie, unable to even consider eating more. He cleared his throat. "Did she say why? Or when she'd be here?"

Deidre reached across the table and squeezed his hand. "No. I'm sorry, Dunc."

He pushed away from the table, his chair scraping the floor. "I'll be in my room."

Duncan took the stairs two at a time. She wasn't coming. And she wasn't taking his calls. Or answering his texts. And she hadn't had the courtesy to talk to him about it. She'd texted his sister. How were they supposed to have a relationship—how were they going to have a business together—if she wouldn't talk to him?

Stripping off his clothes, Duncan turned the water up as hot as it would go and stepped under the spray. Now what? If she wasn't going to talk to him, maybe it was time to force the issue. With five potential new jobs—and he made a mental note to put in return calls to those people this evening—he needed her here and working. His heart ached. He needed her, period.

21

Anna scanned the crowd. Why were airports always so busy? She hitched her backpack higher on her shoulder and pushed through a cluster of people who were walking slower than seemed reasonable.

"Anna!"

She turned, scanning for the person that went with the voice. Aha. Finally. She waved and headed toward her brother. "There you are."

He pulled her into a tight hug. "I could say the same. When you called and said you were flying out, I wondered if we missed April first somewhere along the way. You okay?"

"I don't know, Stu. That's why I'm here."

"For how long?"

"Just 'til tomorrow night."

"Well, Mom's excited to have you. She may not let you go. No chance you're moving out here?"

Anna followed her brother as he wound through the airport. "I...I don't know. Probably not."

"Hmm." Her brother pushed the button for the elevator that would take them to parking. "There's a story there."

"Yeah. Do you mind if I talk to mom and dad about it first?" She wasn't positive she could get through it one time. She certainly didn't need to try twice.

Stuart nodded. "Of course. Come on, let's get you home. Well, to Mom's."

She didn't pay attention on the drive. Just stared out her window, her thoughts circling. Sean's advice on Sunday hadn't been bad. It had certainly given her food for thought. But...was she just scared? Scared of what? Commitment? Using her degree? All she'd known at the end of those questions haunting her sleep for three days was that she needed to see her mom. See her. Not talk on the phone. Not video chat. But in person. So she'd cashed in the airline points she'd been saving for three years and here she was. Hoping to get her head on straight.

"Here we are." Stuart pulled into the driveway of a house Anna recognized only from photos. "I'm going to run home and get Lisa and the kids. We'll be over for dinner after soccer. It's good to see you, Anna."

"Thanks." She pushed open the car door and, with her backpack on her shoulder, strode to the front door.

The door flew open. "Anna!"

Her mother pulled Anna into her arms and squeezed her tight, running her hand over Anna's hair.

"Hi, Mom."

"Come in, come in. You must be exhausted. What time did your flight leave? Do you need to lie down for a little bit?"

Anna smiled, relaxing in to the whirlwind of her mother's love. "I'm good. I...can we just have a cup of coffee and talk?"

Her mom tilted her head to one side and, after a long look, nodded. "Of course, I'll start a fresh pot. Go in the den and give your father a hug. He's missed his baby girl."

Anna dropped her backpack by the hall. Presumably she'd be staying down that way at some point. The den. Where was that? Her mother had disappeared straight ahead, so maybe...Anna turned to the left and shortly found herself in an enormous high-ceilinged room. Her father was stretched out in a recliner with his reading glasses perched on his nose, a book open in his lap.

"There's my baby girl." He patted the arm of his chair. "Come and give me a hug. I'm so glad you came out. Though I wish you could stay longer."

"Hi, Daddy." Anna perched on the edge of the chair's arm and leaned against her dad, wrapping her arm around his neck. "Sorry. I wish that, too. Maybe another time."

"Well, it's good to see you." He slipped his glasses off and looked her over. "You don't look happy. Can I help?"

"I don't know, Dad. I...you want to have coffee with me and Mom?"

He pushed the recliner closed and patted her knee. "You know I never say no to coffee."

Anna followed her dad into the kitchen, where the scent of brewing coffee filled the air. She sat down at the kitchen table and folded her hands in front of her. How did she start?

"Here you go." Anna's mom set a cup of coffee down in front of Anna. "I'll get another cup for you, dear."

She bustled in the kitchen for a few more minutes before sitting down and pouring milk from a pitcher into her mug. "Tell us what's wrong, honey."

Anna's eyes filled. She blinked and reached for the sugar. When she'd stirred her coffee and taken a sip, she launched into a description of the situation with Duncan, the new business, and her conversation with Sean. "I don't know what to do."

"Well, that seems like a two-part problem." Her dad sipped his drink. "The business and Duncan."

"Oh now, honey, I don't think you can separate them like that. She's in love with the boy. How is she supposed to own a business with him if they're not together?"

"I work with people I'm not in love with all the time." He winked.

"I didn't say I wasn't in love with him...I said I didn't know..." Anna ran her hand through her hair. "You're making fun."

"I'm not. Not really." Her father patted her hand. "But I think your mother's closer to the truth than you are. You love him. And that makes it trickier. Unless, of course, he loves you."

He'd said he did. Did she have any reason to doubt it? "He does."

"And is he good at his work? Wait, is this the boy from college? The one you admired but who never liked your ideas?"

Anna nodded. She'd done plenty of complaining about Duncan to her parents in college. But she'd never let on how big a crush she had on him.

"Anna. If you love him, why are you here talking to us instead of there talking to him?" Her mother's voice was quiet, but the disappointment was still evident.

"I don't know. I couldn't think. I needed you." A tear slipped down her cheek.

"You have us. Always. But did you listen to yourself when you were talking? You're excited about this business. And you're in love with Duncan. It seems to me, the best thing you can do is go home and give both of them your best." Anna's mom reached over and squeezed her hand. "But for now, you're here. And I'm glad to have my baby home."

Anna parked and looked up at her apartment building. Well, it wouldn't be hers for long. She'd gotten a call about a sublet while she'd been at her parents' house. It had been the one thing missing that she'd been praying for. Clear direction.

Grabbing her backpack, she pushed open the car door. She'd get a good night's sleep and tomorrow...tomorrow she'd call Duncan and apologize. And pray he'd understand. She'd never thought of herself as someone who was scared and prone to cold feet, but that's exactly what had happened.

"Anna?"

She turned, her brow furrowing. "Duncan?"

He crossed the parking lot, his hands in his pockets. "Hi."

"Hi. What are you doing here?"

"You haven't been returning my calls. Or my texts. So I came to talk to you in person. Only, you weren't here. So I waited."

"You've been waiting for me?"

"Yeah."

She licked her lips. "Come on inside. I was going to call you tomorrow."

"Before we do that, just tell me, are you ending things?" Duncan took a few steps closer.

"No. I'm so sorry, Duncan. For all of it. Come up, okay? I can make some coffee."

He shook his head. "Call me tomorrow then. I should get back. Deidre's been worried."

She frowned, her thoughts scattering all over the place. He'd waited for her all weekend but was just running off now that she was back? She reached out and touched his arm. "I love you, Duncan."

His smile flashed, his teeth gleaming for just a moment in the streetlight. "I love you, too. You look exhausted. We can talk tomorrow. I'm glad you're safe."

He'd been worried about her. Of course he had. She was rude and inconsiderate. "Will you be here?"

"No. I don't think so." Duncan shook his head. "I need to get back. We have clients waiting on designs. Check your email. Call me when you're up."

Her heart ached. Had she damaged things permanently, or was there a way back for them? "First thing. Promise."

"Okay. Get some sleep." He turned and went back to his car.

Anna watched as he drove off and, shoulders slumping, headed inside. She'd call in the morning. But until then, she'd pray. A lot.

22

Duncan hadn't slept very well since Friday. Last night, he probably should've found a hotel in Richmond, but after seeing Anna...it was better to go. She'd looked fine. Happy, even. That was good. But she hadn't jumped in with an explanation of her week-long silence or where she'd been. Maybe she hadn't wanted to get into it in the parking lot, but darn it, he deserved to know, without coffee and small talk first. He hadn't done anything to deserve any of this. Blood thundered in his ears and he took several deep breaths. There was no point in dwelling on it. They'd talk it through when she called and see where it left them.

She'd said she wasn't breaking up with him.

That, at least, kept some of the heaviness from his heart. But what kind of relationship did they have if she didn't trust him enough to talk about what was going on? If all she did was run? There was no future with someone who wouldn't communicate.

"Hey. You okay?" Deidre brought the coffee pot over to the kitchen table and topped off his mug before pouring some in her own. "You got back late last night."

"I don't know. By the time Anna got there, I'd half talked myself into proposing on the spot. Then..."

"Sanity set in?" Deidre shook her head. "You can't propose to someone who just disappears on you, Duncan. You know that. Right?"

"I do. Of course I do." He ran a hand through his hair, but his heart still whispered that he'd made the wrong call to walk away.

"I know that look. You're second guessing yourself. Listen to me. Yes, you knew each other for four years in college. *Ten years ago*. You've known each other now for what, two months? That's fast. Give it time. Once she's here and you're working together every day you'll get a better feel for where things stand and whether or not you want to make her your future."

Duncan took a long drink of coffee and fought the urge to raise his voice. "That's rich, Dee, seeing as how you're engaged to someone you met in March."

Red flooded her face and she pushed back her chair and stood. "You know what? I'm trying to help. Just keep in mind that she didn't even have the courtesy to tell you she wasn't showing up or where she'd be. That's not someone you marry."

"Ever?"

Her shoulders slumped. "No. I didn't mean never. But certainly not until you find out why."

Duncan was saved from answering by his cell phone. Anna's face smiled up at him from the display. "I'll take this outside. I know you mean well. I'll probably appreciate it later."

Deidre shook her head and sat back down.

Duncan tapped the phone's face and held it to his ear as he gathered his coffee and exited the kitchen. "Hello?"

"Hi. It's me. Is...is now a good time?"

"Yeah, of course. So." He trailed off. How was this conversation supposed to go?

"I feel like I need to apologize again."

"What happened? Can you help me understand?" Duncan stepped out of the front door into the thick air of July. Even in the foothills of the Blue Ridge, the humidity of Virginia was alive and well. It might not get as bad as it did in D.C., but it wasn't the cool, crisp air most people associated with living in the mountains. He wandered down the steps and turned, following the path to the sunken garden he'd been working on when Anna had first joined the project in May.

"I'm not sure, exactly. I guess...I got scared."

"Scared? Of what?" Duncan sat on one of the three wrought iron benches he'd put in last week. They were nice finishing touches and made the garden something more than a space to walk through.

"I guess I thought we'd be working together. We hadn't really discussed it—but I imagined it'd be more like college, where we discussed everything as a unit. I wasn't prepared for it not to be like that and...I guess I took that as a sign that you didn't want your name associated with mine. That you were embarrassed by my work and were leaving me to sink on my own."

Duncan set his coffee down beside him and stared at the water trickling out of the fish fountain. He wasn't sure where to start. It seemed ridiculous that she'd jump to that conclusion when the reality was, effectively, exactly the opposite. "I admire your work. I did even in college, though, from what you've said, I went about showing that poorly. You're more than capable of handling projects on your own—just look at the gardens you did here at Peacock Hill if you need any reassurance about that."

"Sure, but weren't you just humoring me? I mean, come on...I'm sure there were changes you would've made if you'd been involved."

"Most likely. But you've admitted already that you redesign landscapes in your head when you see them, right? That doesn't mean it's bad, just that you would've done something differently. I don't think either of us would be happy long-term if we had to run every little decision past the other. Not to mention the fact that we wouldn't be able to take on as many clients. If we want to build a business, one that's going to support us both with a living wage, we can't be stuck in each other's pockets all the time. I trust you to do your job. Can you say the same?"

"Of course I trust you."

Duncan frowned. "There's no 'of course' about it. Not in my mind. I need to know you believe it when you say it."

"I trust you, Duncan. And what you've said makes sense. I...maybe I didn't think it through. I'm sorry."

"It's okay. I want to make sure we're on the same page though. This won't work if we don't talk to each other."

"I'm sorry. You're right."

Duncan closed his eyes. She needed to stop apologizing. "It's not about one of us being right. If you feel strongly that we need to do it the other way, make your case, I'll listen. I'm not trying to steamroll you into doing things my way. I just need to understand what you want."

Anna sighed. "I know that. And I know I made the mess bigger by disappearing—my parents made that clear this weekend when I showed up on their doorstep. I still want to be with you. I still want to do this business with you. But I also understand if you want to back away from either. Or both."

"I don't want that." Duncan took a swig of coffee to ease the burning acid in his throat. She'd run all the way to California rather than talk to him? At least she'd come back. "On either count."

"Okay. I'm glad. I was thinking I could bring a car load of stuff down each day this week. My sublet won't move in until Saturday. I'm leaving all the furniture though, as part of the agreement."

"Furniture we have. There's enough in the basement to outfit a room for you and then some. That shouldn't be an issue. Do you think you'll have time to contact three of the five clients I sent you information on last night?"

"Yeah. I can do that before I load up the car. The first three looked the most doable for me?"

He'd put them in that order because he'd thought the same, but he wanted to give her the option to choose whatever sounded interesting. "Okay. I'll contact the bottom two. Do you think you can stay for dinner tonight, before you head back? I'd like to spend some time with you...I've missed you."

"I'd like that." There was a smile in her voice and a warmth that had been lacking until now. "I should be there by lunch."

Duncan ended the call and leaned back, stretching his legs out in front of him. He sipped his coffee and watched the water as it spilled out of the fish's mouth and splashed off the scales and fins that were artfully rendered in the concrete. Why did it feel like they'd taken five steps backward and only one or two to the front?

Anna knocked on the door frame of the front room and stepped in. "Hi."

Duncan saved his design and looked up from his laptop. His heart leapt in his chest. It was good to see her in the daylight, though the circles under her eyes that he'd noticed the night before were still there. He smiled. "Hi, yourself."

Anna twisted her fingers together and took a hesitant step into the room. "Deidre said everyone's using this room as an office right now. It's a nice space."

"Yeah. And flexible." He gave himself a mental kick. Why was this so hard? It was like they hardly knew each other anymore. He pushed back his chair and stood. "It's good to see you."

"Oh, Duncan." Anna flung herself across the room and into his arms, burying her face in his chest. "I'm so sorry."

He wrapped his arms around her and rubbed her back as his shirt grew damp. "Shh. Hey. It's okay. Anna."

She shook her head. "It's not okay. How can it be?"

Duncan kissed her forehead and tipped her chin up so he could see her face. "Because it is. I love you. We hit a bump. We got through it. As long as we communicate with each other, we'll be okay."

Anna wiped her eyes and nodded. "Okay. I missed you."

"Well then, it seems like the simple thing to do is not run away again."

She chuckled and leaned up, pressing her lips to his.

It was as if fingers that had been squeezing his heart relaxed and allowed it to beat freely again for the first time in a week. Duncan held her, returning the kiss, reveling in the sensation of having her in his arms again.

"I just need—oops. Sorry." Claire cleared her throat.

Anna blushed and looked away.

Duncan loosened his hold, but didn't completely let go. His sister had to know he'd kissed girls before. "You need me?"

"No. The printer. Um. I was hoping I could use your web browser real quick?"

Duncan gestured to his laptop. "Be my guest. Just don't mess with my design program."

"Just the web browser. Promise." Claire dropped into the chair and clicked.

Duncan looked at Anna. "Need help unloading your car?"

"Sure. That'd be great."

23

Anna grabbed the lightweight short-sleeved sweater that went with her knit tank top and checked the mirror. She'd dressed up her jeans a little with the fancier top, but it was still casual. The church here was casual though. People wore a wide variety of clothes. And she'd never felt the need to fuss this much before. Just get downstairs and quit making people wait. Not people. Duncan. Deidre and Claire were probably long gone.

She hurried down the stairs, barely noticing the stained-glass window that usually kept her so enraptured that every step was slow and deliberate.

"Ready?"

"Yeah. Sorry." Anna crossed the foyer to the front door that Duncan held open. "We're not late, are we?"

"Not yet. We should be fine. And if we are, well, Mrs. Patterson will let us know afterward."

Anna chuckled.

Duncan smiled and kissed her cheek as he opened her car door. "You look nice."

"Thanks." Somewhere over the past week, they'd found their stride again. The first couple of days had been rocky. Most of that was her fault. It was hard to forgive herself for her behavior. It had been childish and ridiculous and a whole bunch of other adjectives that she was trying to stop replaying in her mind. Duncan had put it behind him. She needed to do the same.

The trip down the hill to town was lovely, as always. Wildflowers bloomed on the sides of the road, seemingly oblivious to the summer heat. Even in town, neat rows of flowers lined the walkways to houses or businesses. How had she missed all the color before?

The parking lot was full, but a handful of people still milled around on the church's front porch. She let out a breath. Not late.

"See? Right on time." Duncan found a spot at the back of the lot and parked his car. "And you were worried."

Anna laughed. "But not you, right?"

He held his fingers a tiny bit apart. "Maybe a little."

As they crossed the lot, Duncan took her hand. She gave it a light squeeze. Would there always be that initial thrill of shivers when they touched, or would it wear off over time? It didn't matter. The quiet, steady reassurance that came from the contact was enough.

"You made it. I was beginning to wonder. Deidre and Claire were here in time to help set up the coffee, you know." Mrs. Patterson greeted them as they entered the building. "Have you decided where you'd like to serve, now that you're coming here regularly?"

Duncan shook his head and took a bulletin. "Not yet, ma'am. Is there a list of needs I could look over?"

"Nothing so formal." The older woman sniffed. "I take it you haven't paid much attention to the pathetic attempts at flower beds that currently grace the property as you zip in and out of the parking lot?"

Anna pressed her lips together to keep from laughing. "Is there a grounds team we could join?"

"Team?" Mrs. Patterson shook her head. "Right now there's just Old Joe and his water hose, when he remembers to go dribble a few precious drops on the poor withering husks out there."

"Who would we speak to about that?" Duncan smiled.

"The pastor, of course. Just catch him at the end of the service. There's probably even a little money we can send your way if it's needed. Not a lot, mind you, so nothing fancy, but I do miss having tulips in the spring." Mrs. Patterson nodded to emphasize her words and then shooed them toward the sanctuary doors. "You'd best get a seat. See you talk to the pastor."

"I guess I know where we're serving." Duncan's eyes danced with humor.

"Guess so. Always good to get strong suggestions. But in this case, I can't say I mind since she didn't point us toward dinner prep on Wednesday nights or something. I can get around in the kitchen, but it's not really my strong suit." Anna slid into the pew with a nod to Deidre, Jeremiah, and Claire.

Claire tapped her wrist with an exaggerated stern face.

Duncan rolled his eyes.

Anna smiled. Claire's sense of humor was hard to get a handle on. Anna was reasonably sure she was joking, and Duncan's response made that seem more likely, but still...it was like getting caught doing something naughty.

As they sang, Anna looked around the sanctuary. It already seemed more like a church home than the church she'd attended in Richmond for so many years. Sure, she had a handful of friends there. Sean, for one, and...well, Sean mostly. She was grateful God had landed her here, with Duncan and his sisters, and even Mrs. Patterson.

During the sermon, she flipped over her notes and sketched an outline of the church property to the best of her memory. It'd be nice to have something a little different—something beyond the strip of bushes on either side of the building. Was there room for a prayer garden somewhere? Maybe it could separate the playground from the parking lot—that might be more visually appealing as people approached the church. They could do a small prayer walk in stone pavers for the floor and put in some alcoves with benches. Maybe add a more mature tree to provide partial shade. Not too close to the church building, just in case there was a big storm and it got knocked down.

Duncan's elbow dug into her ribs.

Anna looked up, her face heating, and stood with everyone else for the closing song. She'd completely missed the sermon. Did they have any way to listen during the week?

As the organ started up, Duncan nodded toward her paper. "I like it. But what's the little square area?"

"Prayer garden? I did one at my church in Richmond. People seemed to like it."

"Nice." Duncan grinned. "Maybe we could put those tulips in the front beds for Mrs. P?"

"Yeah."

"Hey." Jeremiah slid past Deidre and Claire. "You can stream the recording on the church website. Usually by Tuesday afternoon."

Anna winced. "Sorry."

Jeremiah laughed. "Don't be. I've needed it myself a time or two. What were you sketching?"

"Mrs. Patterson suggested that we might want to volunteer to be the grounds team. I had an idea that I wanted to get down before..."

"Cool. Old Joe isn't up to much anymore. But try to include him? He's been keeping things nice since I was a kid. I'd hate to see him left out."

Anna nodded. That was the last thing she wanted. "I'll make sure of it. Have you ever done a sprinkler system?"

"Good idea." Duncan tilted his head so he could see the drawing. "I know the basics, but I wouldn't want to do it all."

"I've done a couple, yeah. Just let me know when." Jeremiah tapped the paper. "This is good. Talk to the pastor on your way out. You're coming to Mom and Dad's for lunch, right?"

Were they? Anna looked at Duncan, who was nodding. "We'll be there as soon as we're done here."

Anna double-checked her folder one final time before stepping out of the car. She'd dressed up her jeans with a pink silk blouse, but Duncan had assured her that no client expected a landscape proposal to be presented in a skirted suit. It didn't sit right, but he had to know more than she did. After all, she'd spent the last ten years answering reference desk questions. Sean's reprimand about selling herself short flitted through her mind and she swallowed. Okay. She'd done some small jobs for friends. This was...different. Even the work at Peacock Hill had been easier than this. If Deidre had asked her to go, sure, she would've been upset at the lost opportunity, but it was like she'd spent time putting her heart into a design.

She'd made it to the front door without even noticing the yard as it existed currently. Not smart. She'd visited once last week and taken the photos and measurements she'd used for the drawings, but still. Preoccupation was never a good thing. Time to get her head in the game. Anna raised her hand and knocked.

After what seemed like an eternity, a young woman balancing a small child on her hip pulled open the door. "Can I help you?"

"Hi. I'm Anna Hamilton? We had an appointment to go over the landscaping proposal?"

"Is that today? That's Wednesday, I thought."

Anna nodded. "Today's Wednesday."

"It can't be." A wail started up somewhere in the house and the woman turned with a groan. "Come on in, I'm not sure what those two are doing, but it's obviously nothing good. Do you mind sitting in the kitchen?"

Anna closed her mouth without responding. The mom had already left. This was off to a stellar start. She pulled open the storm door and stepped into the house. She checked to make sure it latched behind her before eyeing the main door. Close it? Leave it? It was closed before so...Anna pushed it closed as well and followed the sounds of crying kids and end-of-her-rope mother that came from the back of the house.

"I put the TV on for them. I don't usually do that during the day but sometimes it's better all-around. And that gave me a chance to check the calendar and confirm that yes, somewhere in the midst of twin three-year-olds with ear infections, I lost a day. I'm so sorry. Can I get you some coffee or something?" The woman was already pouring a mug from the carafe on the kitchen counter.

"Sure. Thanks. Do we need to reschedule?" Please say no.

The woman waved her hand and grabbed another mug from the cupboard above the sink. "It's never any better. Three under four will do that for you. Most days I wouldn't trade it for the world, but they keep me running. Please sit. Cream and sugar? And did I tell you to call me Lorelei or did that escape me, too? 'Cause honestly, if you'll just talk to me in long sentences about something that isn't animated, I'll let you do whatever you want with the yard."

Anna laughed and took a seat at the kitchen table, carefully scooping something—oatmeal, maybe—off the surface with a napkin before setting down her folder. "Cream and sugar are great, thanks. And I'll try to remember to use the Latin names for the flowers whenever possible. Although some of them sound like they could be anime characters."

Lorelei grinned. "I knew I liked you. Randy did too. It's too bad y'all aren't based here in Charlottesville. I think you and I could be friends."

Anna smiled, her heart warming. "Well, I'm not that far off and I've been known to make a drive for a friend now and then."

"Really?" Lorelei clapped her hands, brought the coffees over, and sat. She propped her elbow in a puddle of something pink and, from how it clung when she tried to move her arm, gooey. With barely a sigh, she wiped her arm and nodded to the folder. "I can't wait any more. Plus, the show they're watching is only like forty minutes long. So...don't keep me in suspense. Please."

Anna laughed and opened the folder. Lorelei was a hoot. And she'd certainly managed to put Anna at ease. Maybe they could become friends—Anna was racking up more of those than she'd had in a long time. It felt good. Maybe, just maybe, things were going to be all right. She drew out the top page and spun it so Lorelei got the full effect before launching into her description.

Her blouse was sticking to her, and her hair...there would be no more looking at her hair until after she'd had a shower. She'd made the mistake of checking it in the car when she'd arrived at her second consultation's house and all that had done was make her incredibly self-conscious. She'd thrown it into a ponytail, but that could only do so much once it started to try and curl. Even with all of that, she couldn't stop the grin that split her face.

"I don't even have to ask how it went. Congratulations." Duncan crossed the foyer and picked her up, spinning in a little circle. "I didn't doubt you for a minute."

"I did. But you know what? I shouldn't have. They're both eager to get started, made only tiny tweaks, and Lorelei may end up becoming a friend. I think you'd like her husband. She suggested maybe we could go on a double-date sometime if she could talk her mom into babysitting." Anna laughed and pressed a smacking kiss to Duncan's lips. "Thank you."

"For what? I didn't do anything. You did it." Duncan set her down but continued holding her close.

"You believed in me." Anna looked up and held his gaze. "I couldn't even believe in myself, but you did."

One corner of his mouth curved up. "That was easy. You're talented and smart and beautiful."

Her heart took off at a gallop and her arms tightened around his waist as she breathed out a prayer of thanksgiving for Duncan's presence in her life. She didn't deserve him or his love. But now that she had him, she wasn't letting him get away, either. "I love you."

"I love you, too." He lowered his lips to hers for a brief but thorough kiss. "Come on, Claire made dinner and it smells amazing."

Anna stepped back and inhaled. A rich, meaty scent hung in the air. How had she missed that? "I need a shower first. I'm begging you."

He laughed. "Go on, then. But don't take too long. I'm starved."

Chuckling, Anna jogged to the stairs. She paused at the bottom step to look over her shoulder at him. He made quite a picture in the t-shirt and jeans that showed off his muscles. Her mouth watered and she forced herself up the stairs. He loved her. She loved him. They'd talked marriage a few times...now that she was ready, how long would he make her wait?

24

Duncan printed the end-of-month reports and sighed. Two months under their belts. Ten satisfied clients in the books and a handful of consultations booked for the upcoming month of September. Not a bad start at all. And they ought to be able to continue working into at least early November, which would let them build up some money to tide them over until spring when projects picked up again. Although, he had a few ideas of what might convince people to at least start planning over the winter. If they could keep a little design work flowing, it would help.

"You about done in here?" Deidre poked her head around the corner with a frown. "Anna's friend Sean is on his way down today, remember? He's going to look over the spaces and suggest furniture layouts."

"Right. How's the office setup in the basement coming along?" He collected the papers from the printer and closed his laptop lid. "I can move the rest of this down there if the room's clear."

"It's clear enough. That'd be a big help. The painter is supposed to come today, too." Deidre tugged on her ponytail. "And if the two of them have positive things to say, then I really need to sit down with Jeremiah tonight and set a wedding date. He's anxious to get the show on the road. So am I."

Duncan smiled, ignoring the pang in his chest. His sister was getting married. How did she get to be old enough for that?

"Any thoughts on when you and Anna might be doing the same thing?"

His eyebrows lifted. "Weren't you just counseling me about not rushing into anything?"

She huffed out a breath. "Two months ago. Duncan, even Mrs. Patterson at church is beginning to wonder if you're just leading her on."

"Oh, well, if Mrs. Patterson is worried."

"You know what I'm saying. What's stopping you?" Deidre glanced into the hall before moving to stand beside him and rest a hand on his arm. "Is something wrong?"

Nothing was wrong. In fact, it was as close to perfect as he could imagine. He shook his head. "We've been busy. Once word got out about what we were doing...we've been scrambling to keep up."

"That's a good problem to have."

He nodded. "Things will be slowing down soon and then—"

"Don't wait too long, okay? You don't want her to think you've changed your mind."

Anna didn't think that, did she? They went for walks in the moonlight out by the lake or through the gardens almost every night. Most of that time was spent discussing the future they wanted to build together. "Did she say something?"

Deidre shook her head. "But I don't want you to accidentally hurt her, either."

"I'll keep that in mind." Duncan carried his laptop to the printer and balanced it on top while he unhooked the cables. He picked up the two pieces of equipment and aimed for the door. "I'll get the printer hooked back up when it's downstairs."

Deidre nodded and glanced at her phone as she disappeared into the formal dining room.

Was he waiting too long? Duncan crossed the foyer and pulled open the door to the basement stairs. He'd been busy with the landscaping business, and with helping Deidre with a few projects around Peacock Hill. She'd decided to get everything else finished before bringing in the detail painter. There'd been fancy art on plaster in a handful of other rooms—not just the breakfast room—and Deidre wanted it all done at the same time. Which made sense. He pushed the door at the bottom of the stairs and nudged the light switch with his elbow. Fluorescent lights flickered to life down the length of the hallway.

The basement still needed something to give it some warmth. The plain corporate grey Berber on the floor did nothing but keep the floor from being freezing. If it was just going to be offices and the girls' living spaces, that'd be one thing, but Deidre had decided to make a business center for guests down here as well. And the charm level was significantly lacking.

"Hey. Is that why it's saying the printer's offline?" Anna grinned as Duncan set the machine down on the table in what was rapidly transforming into the shared office space slash business center.

"That would be why. I'll get it hooked right up. Deidre's itching to have the main floor clear for Sean to look over. I guess he's coming today?"

Anna nodded. "It'll be good to see him. He emails me now and then, probing for details—I think he's anxious to get some events booked out here."

That seemed like a stretch. Richmond wasn't horribly far, but there had to be conference centers closer that would do the same trick? Then again, wasn't Deidre banking on it being the opposite? He plugged in the printer and checked the settings. Looked like everything held. "Give that a try?"

After a second, the printer clicked and whirred before spitting out several pieces of paper.

Anna reached for them. "Thanks."

Duncan frowned. "What are those?"

Anna blushed. "Just some ideas I had for the groundskeeper's cottage that's out past the lake. I was going to talk to Deidre about it, see what her plans are."

"I imagine she and Jeremiah will live out there, won't they?"

Anna shook her head. "They'll live down here once they're married. She wants to be in the main building in case anyone needs her during a retreat type event. That's why her space is set up a lot like a two-bedroom apartment while Claire and I are sharing the smaller space."

"It's that bad, sharing with Claire?" Duncan didn't consider either of his sisters particularly hard to live with, but he also had never paid that much attention. And he'd been out of the house when they were in high school.

"No. It's fine. I just thought when we—you and I—are married that it might be nicer..." Anna trailed off and cleared her throat. "Maybe I'll put these away until later. If Sean's coming today, Deidre has a lot on her plate anyway."

Smiling, Duncan took two steps to close the distance between them. "You're planning a nest? For us?"

She looked away. "It's stupid. And presumptuous. I realize that. So you don't need to make fun of me."

Duncan put a finger under her chin and turned her face back so their eyes met. "I'm not making fun. I'm flattered. And relieved."

"Relieved?"

He nodded. His insides were jumping around like deranged grasshoppers. "This isn't how I thought I'd do this."

Anna paled and her eyes grew wide.

Duncan sank to one knee still holding both her hands in his. "Anna Hamilton, I love you. Would you do me the very big honor of becoming my wife?"

Anna let out a strangled laugh. "You're serious?"

He nodded. "Incredibly. Though I don't have a ring yet. And in my mind, I had us out to a fancy dinner in Charlottesville or something...I was working on it. Do you want me to figure it out and try again?"

"No."

He frowned and the air in the room seemed to disappear. "No?"

"Yes."

Duncan searched her face. What was the yes and what was the no? His confusion must've been obvious because Anna's hand flew to her mouth and she sank to her knees in front of him.

"I love you, Duncan. Yes, I'll marry you. No, you don't have to do something big and fancy. That isn't us." Her hands slid around his neck and she gave a gentle pull, bringing his lips closer to hers.

"I love you."

She leaned forward until their breath mingled. "Duncan?"

"Yeah?"

"Shut up and kiss me."

He'd known since college that Anna had good ideas. It only seemed reasonable to do what she said and follow through. He lowered his lips to hers and thanked God for bringing them together again, this time in a season where their love could bloom.

Want a free book?

If you enjoyed *A Heart Reclaimed* and would like to read another book of mine, you can receive a free novel, simply by signing up for my newsletter here: http://bit.ly/2g0AGvf

Look for *A Heart Realigned*, book 3 in the Peacock Hill Romance series, coming soon!

Author's Note

Thank you for reading *A Heart Reclaimed!* I hope that you enjoyed getting to know Duncan and Anna. I would appreciate it if you'd help others enjoy it too by leaving a review and telling your friends about it. Any success my books have is owed to readers like you who take the time to tell others about my stories. Thank you, from the bottom of my heart. Duncan and Anna (along with Deidre and Jeremiah from the first book in the Peacock Hill Romance series, A Heart Restored) will continue to appear in future installments of the stories set at Peacock Hill. I hope you'll continue to join me in exploring that lovely old house in the mountains.

I continue to owe a huge debt of gratitude to my husband and sons for giving me the time to write, my sister for her unflinching support and encouragement, and my critique partners Heather Gray, Jan Elder, and Valerie Comer. More than anything, I'm grateful that God continues to give me words and makes it possible for me to write them down.

I'd love to hear from you! You can connect with me on Facebook

(www.Facebook.com/ElizabethMaddrey)

my webpage (www.ElizabethMaddrey.com) or via email. To stay current with news and occasional giveaways, please subscribe to my newsletter (links on Facebook or my webpage).

About the Author

Elizabeth Maddrey began writing stories as soon as she could form the letters properly and has never looked back. Though her practical nature and love of computers, math, and organization steered her into computer science at Wheaton College, she always had one or more stories in progress to occupy her free time. This continued through a Master's program in Software Engineering, several years in the computer industry, teaching programming at the college level, and a Ph.D. in Computer Technology in Education. When she isn't writing, Elizabeth is a voracious consumer of books and has mastered the art of reading while undertaking just about any other activity.

Elizabeth is the author of more than ten books, both fiction and non-fiction. She lives in the suburbs of Washington, D.C. with her husband and their two incredibly active little boys.